# STORIES
# OF A
# HANGMAN

## Ryan Surprise

2021 White Bird Publications, LLC

Copyright © 2021 by Ryan Surprise
Cover design by Ryan Surprise

Published in the United States
by White Bird Publications, LLC, Austin, Texas
www.whitebirdpublications.com

ISBN 978-1-63363-515-9
eBook ISBN 978-1-63363-516-6
Library of Congress Control Number: 2021932837

PRINTED IN THE UNITED STATES OF AMERICA

## *Dedication*

To Faith.

# Table of Contents

To Theresa,

from the man you
hardly knew

Ryan S

# STORIES
# OF A
# HANGMAN

**White Bird
Publications**

# *Prologue*

My father was a hangman, and he taught me his trade. I was too young to remember much before he started taking me with him to execute the guilty. I remember my mother died giving birth to my brother. I remember the glow of a lantern and the hours of screams. When the house grew silent, my father lifted me with his strong hands and took me away. I can hardly remember her face now. One day I had a mother, and after that day, I didn't anymore.

We would travel to the towns around Cheyenne for the executions. During my earlier years, I would hand him the supplies. But as I grew older, he'd let me build the gallows with him. After my mother passed, his black hair turned gray. By the time I was a man he had stark white hair and a short beard around his mouth. His muscles lost their mass and his eyes were never the same, like orbs sunk in glossy film.

At some of the towns we would visit, there would be mothers, wives, and widows shouting in front of saloons about drunkenness and depravity. This confused me as a boy; I had grown up in saloons and inns, after all. We rarely stayed at our home on the outskirts of Cheyenne for more than a month. Sometimes we would take the carriage into town or trains across the state for executions. Thankfully, my father knew to hide me away as soon as we entered an inn. I was fast asleep before the prostitutes found their men.

When I learned about that sort of thing, my father would often keep me at home. Most of my memories of that house were of being alone. Without a mother or brothers, I had nothing to do aside from chores. The house was a shack by the time I was a man; the weather and wind had torn at it bit by bit. My father never painted it since I was born. It kept the cold out in the winter.

There weren't many hangings in the winters of my youth. The heat is what does it to some people. The winters of the Wyoming Territory set people's minds right about what's important. The cold forces us to rely on one another, and the snow makes it harder to run away. It settles our rage and makes us look to each other for warmth. With those long winters, reading was the best way to pass the time.

My father grew so tired of me at home that he sent me to school. Ms. McGivney was a pale slip of a thing with red hair that twirled down her head. I remember her face with the sunlight reaching over it as she looked at me. My education was unusual. My father would often take me away for executions, so I missed the lessons. I rarely studied with the other children in the schoolhouse. She often taught me on my own. It was a great burden on her part, not that she noticed.

Most children go to school to read and write, but Ms. McGivney saw past the ordinary concentrations of society. She taught me to appreciate the finer things. She introduced me to books of the best writers and the best poetry.

"It isn't just about reading the newspaper and learning more about the world," she said. "It's about imagining what can happen and how to do it." These lofty ideas stayed with me all my life. She saved me from the boredom of work that seemed to seep into my bones as I grew older. Edgar taught me loyalty. Poe taught me about evil, and Paul taught me about virtue. Thomas Paine taught me to yearn for more, and George Washington taught me responsibility. In the end, they all inspired me to strive before I had to prove myself.

At sixteen, my father believed that I'd had more than enough learning. I never said goodbye to Ms. McGivney. I never returned to the schoolhouse. Eventually, in my mind, she became only a face from a prairie school.

Because of my uncommon education, my mind was always at work, always wondering. This was agitating to both my father and me when he would take me with him for the next execution. My father never let me see the hangings as a boy. He would lock me in our rented room and made sure that the inn or saloon wasn't facing the center of town where the executions took place.

He'd say, "It's not fit for you," or "You're not fit for it yet." That didn't stop me from trying. When I was young and bored stiff in my cage, I would try to see what was happening outside. Mostly, there would be nobody around. The streets would be empty, and I could see the edge of a crowd only sometimes. The first time I saw a hanging was when I was still a boy.

The saloon my father chose to stay in was very old. Its doors had no locks. He tried to trick me by commanding me to sleep. He scratched at the door with the keys to our home, pretending that he locked me in. I knew where he had built the gallows. We always assembled them together. That time there were three thieves who had been captured. I snuck away into a stable that looked down the main street of the town. My palms were sweaty, and my hand shook as I pulled myself into the threshold of the dark stables. The horses stamped their feet and brushed themselves with their tails. I found the window that had the clearest view of the ceremony.

I tried to silently climb near the window to see. The gallows were far away. I could see the three men standing above the heads of the crowd. They had burlap sacks over their heads. There were murmurs from the crowd and some instructions from the sheriff or some voice of authority beyond them. I waited for a long time, and then, suddenly, they weren't standing anymore. The crowd cheered. They just fell, like they disappeared. It was finished before I could notice. On later recollections, I began to understand how quickly life could go. Despite the ceremony, three lives were extinguished in the blink of an eye. My later experiences would prove that true.

Knowing what had happened, I did not try to see any more hangings unless my father agreed. I sat on the bed of our room until he had finished his work. He knocked on the door to wake me. I sat there quietly and looked up at him as he stood in the threshold.

"We'll go home tonight," he said. I tried to see if he knew what I had seen. I couldn't tell from his eyes what he knew or didn't know. I stepped from the bed and headed to the carriage. We didn't speak on the trip home that day. We had a silent dinner of what we could muster and went to bed. I never asked if he knew all along.

Eventually, I would become a hangman too. This story began on a cool October day with fog in the streets. I was seventeen. My father and I had stayed the night after a hanging. I remember waking to the sound of my father's ire. I half expected it to be a dream, but I looked out the window and saw that he was standing in the street. I couldn't see who he was roaring at, but I watched him walk into the general store. His fists clenched; his shoulders tightened. He wrenched the door off its hinges like it was the last barrier to a spring and he was dying of thirst. The lanterns on the street still burned. They looked like little suns in the mist.

My head snapped to the door when I heard the gunfire. The second shot lit the room for an instant. I got out of bed and frantically searched through my father's possessions. He had a revolver. He must have hidden it in the room somewhere. I threw the mattress off the bed and thought of scratching at the nails in the floorboards to find it. I fell onto the ground when I realized. There was only one thing to believe. There were more pulses through the window. I crawled to it and looked down. My father stood in the street with his head hanging back, looking to the heavens. He wore a delighted expression. He was happy to do it.

He fired the remaining bullets into the road that split the town. Nobody was there. He just did it for his own amusement. The sheriff and his deputy rode in on their horses, and my father let the pistol fall out of his hand. He never stopped smiling. After they chained him in the street, I watched them take him to the sheriff's office. A great weight pulled my shoulders down as I stepped out of the inn. My father, protector, and companion had abandoned his duty to me. I had to pick up the yoke for our family of two.

I walked into the sheriff's office and saw my father lying in a cell. The sheriff saw me and stood up. He towered over me, and I knew not to do anything to wind up in that cell with him.

"Get out of here, son," the sheriff warned. My father said nothing. I ignored the sheriff and wrapped my hands around the cell bars. The sheriff's deputy stepped forward to show me out. My father didn't move; he didn't even raise his head. I rushed past the deputy, not looking back. Feeling pity for me, the deputy stopped by the inn to let me know when the trial would begin.

Like most buildings in that town, the courthouse was designed for a small congregation. The clean, wooden floor was less than twenty steps wide. The musty heat hung in the air like cigar smoke, and the red-faced judge squinted down at my father for the entirety of his trial. I hated the sight of him with his blubbery cheeks pressing his eyes against my father. That judge would send more men to the gallows than any in the territory. The general store owner's widow wept from across the room. I tried not to look. I felt some shame for my father. It was a speedy trial, as designed. The only words he uttered during his trial were "guilty."

A cloudless sky stood behind my father at the gallows. The rope sat around his neck. His wet, downcast eyes never met mine. I don't think he looked at anyone. The executioner asked him if he had any last words, his stillness unmoved. My arms shook in their sleeves. Say something, I thought. *Tell me why! Give me a reason!*

The sack ran over his face. When they threw the lever to break my father's neck, I still hoped he would answer. I was disappointed. I've always tried to remember his face on that day. Maybe one day it will reveal to me what he was thinking, either on that day or the day he killed that man.

When I was young, I used to believe that evil was fixed. However, as I grew older, I saw that it is strange and ever changing. Even the best of us can fall. Even those who believe in the law are punished for their unexpected infractions. My father was one of those men. The men he hanged weren't like him, but he died the same way they did, for his sins, his crimes, and for justice in a dying world.

## The Hanging of a Drunkard

Most folks are happy that drunkenness isn't a crime, especially men. In most of the places I've been, drunkenness is the cornerstone of all other sins. Gambling away the family lot, unwholesome speech, licentiousness, brawling, and at the end, the drunkenness itself. Most drunkards are habitual, but not the one I most remember. This story isn't about the sin of drink or about temperance. It's the story of a boy and his bottle.

In Chugwater Bluff, two boys left their farms after dinner, letting the dying, pale red sky guide their dark figures to a dirt path between their homesteads. Their cheerful whispers shot out into the cool evening air. The night was ripe for their first step towards manhood. They could feel it, in the sunlight and their drawn back shoulders. They shared their excitement as they joyfully marched to the town saloon.

Chugwater Bluff was made up of a general store, a pub, and a church, perched on a plateau above a dozen farms that were scattered below. That town was an outpost away from Cheyenne and the railroad that connected it to civilization. The two boys were sixteen years old. The age of majority was mostly ignored in this territory.

The saloon owner, Mr. Salisbury, was an old man with a crooked eye and a crooked way of doing business. He made most of his drinks personally with stained jars in the storeroom. The swill he sold was always in stock when he ran out of cash for his suppliers. He was a sad man, really. He lost his wife and children in a divorce while he was fighting with the 84th Regiment from Indiana. His eye looked crooked on account of a cannon shell that exploded near his face. He survived to be remembered by nobody in the town where he was raised. He didn't bother traveling over the Rocky Mountains. He just stayed in Chugwater Bluff.

With the general store selling liquor as well, the saloon was empty most nights. The only company

Mr. Salisbury had was that of the occasional cowboys from the northern territories. The most excitement he had since coming to town was when some ranchers from Calgary visited his saloon. They loved his service and tall tales, although they didn't have the heart to tell him his drinks tasted like poison. The lack of excitement in that small, new town was the downfall of those boys.

That night, Harris Townsend and Gilbert McCrery entered the saloon with youthful confidence. Mr. Salisbury was ready for a short night. Nobody had visited him in several days. He was checking if the cash register still opened when the pair walked through the door.

"Two shots of whiskey, please," Harris said. His high-pitched voice almost made Mr. Salisbury laugh. His crooked eye shifted towards the door.

"Come on in," he said. The boys pulled up two stools and sat. The saloon was cramped and full of dust. The bar took up most of the building's interior. There were two small tables behind the boys. That saloon didn't have a full house for some time. Mr. Salisbury curtly poured them two shots of whiskey, as they'd asked.

"Thank you, sir," they said.

"Twenty cents, then," he said with his palm

facing up. The boys each planted a dime in his hand. He smiled his sharp-toothed, cracked smile and tossed them into the cash register. Harris and Gilbert talked as they tasted their first whiskeys, and Mr. Salisbury played with his bar towel as they finished.

"How about another round?" Harris asked, waving his glass. Mr. Salisbury kept an eye on the door. It was a quiet night. There wasn't anyone around except for those boys and the stars. He set the towel on his shoulder and poured them another drink. He took their dimes and dropped them into the cash register.

As the night wore on, Harris felt his head bobble, weightless, realizing this sudden, new feeling made him laugh loudly. Even Salisbury was becoming friendly. Harris and Gilbert couldn't speak clearly, but they didn't need to. As his eyes rose up in laughter, Harris caught the shine of Mr. Salisbury's service revolver. The weapon hung on the wall above the mirror behind the bar. He looked back at Gilbert before Mr. Salisbury could see him admiring it.

"I'll be right back," Mr. Salisbury said. He walked into the storeroom, and the door slapped shut. Harris took Gilbert by the arm. Gilbert's smile dropped as his friend's grip tightened. Harris squinted his eyes; he tried to focus on his one friend in the middle.

"I want that gun," Harris said.

"What?"

"Let's think of a way to distract him." The door swung open. Mr. Salisbury slid another bottle between the boys. Gilbert glanced from Harris to the bottle. Harris could feel the moisture spread beneath his hands on the bar.

"There isn't much left. Ten cents," Mr. Salisbury said with a shake of the bottle. Harris's teeth chattered as he reached for another dime. A sudden chill twisted around his body. Gilbert just watched his friend reach in his pocket. Once the dime lay on the table, Gilbert knew he should lay another down too.

"You boys know how to hold your own, eh?" Harris let the shot of whiskey slide down his throat. Gilbert watched his friend and imitated his movements. His nerves wrenched any sense from his head.

Once the empty whiskey bottle came down on the bar, the boys got to thinking. Mr. Salisbury threw the bottle away and pressed his hands together as he waited for their next order. Harris looked at Gilbert.

Gilbert looked at Mr. Salisbury, and Harris looked at Mr. Salisbury's gun. An idea flicked in Gilbert's mind.

"Do you have anything stronger?" Gilbert asked.

Mr. Salisbury nodded. "Sure, I do. It'll be fifteen cents, though."

Gilbert nodded. Harris instinctively put some nickels on the table. Mr. Salisbury didn't move at first. He stayed a while. The boys watched him. He kept his back against the wall as he moved toward the door to his storeroom. He seemed to have a suspicion that they were up to no good. He turned quickly to face the door and walked into the next room. Harris sprang to the top of the bar and reached for the revolver. He plucked it from its stead and opened the chamber to see six bullets inside. He ran off out the door and Gilbert followed as fast as his numbed feet could go.

"You damned scoundrels!" They heard Mr. Salisbury cry from the saloon as they raced from Chugwater Bluff. Their cool sweat slipped against their arms and their hot breath flew past them in the night air. They ran almost a quarter mile before they stopped. They were so tired, and with bellies full of whiskey, they had no endurance to speak of. It was a clear night sky with the moonlight shining over them.

They looked at the revolver with unblinking eyes. They examined its every mark and feature. Gilbert looked around and saw a lantern hanging on a porch of a nearby farmhouse.

"Bet you can't hit that from here," he said. Harris scoffed and planted his feet. The layers of darkness tricked his eyes, and his whiskey-soaked vision couldn't keep the lantern in place for more than a moment. He held up the revolver in both hands and pulled the hammer back with his thumbs. At last his vision was clear, or so he thought.

His first shot missed, and the sound scared the two of them. The great spark of light made it difficult to see, quickly swallowing the scene in darkness again. Harris pulled the hammer back again and fired. The lantern didn't move. He wrenched the hammer back again, shifted his feet inside his boots, and fired away.

His smile ran off his face once he heard a mother's cry. The horrid wail rushed from the house and filled the bluff. Harris and Gilbert ran back to their houses, they thought. It was still too dark to see. It must have been the way, any direction where they couldn't hear her screams.

Harris forced his hand against the front door of his family home and scattered up the steps to his bedroom. Sweating, exhausted and scared, he crawled into bed, shaking until he couldn't stay awake any longer. The woman's trembling moans laid out the horror that would arise that dawn.

The marshals were summoned to Chugwater Bluff that night. A neighbor rode his horse down to Cheyenne and brought them back to town. When the marshals arrived, they saw three holes in the side of the house. The mother grieved in a bedroom with her husband holding her arms. Her shoulders shuddered and her face was covered in streams of tears. The marshal found their only daughter lying in bed, bleeding from the heart.

The marshals arrived at the Townsend farm with certainty settling on their shoulders. They weren't happy, but they found their man. Harris Townsend was lying in his bed when they knocked for him. His father, Roger, answered the door.

"We're looking for a boy named Harris Townsend," the marshal said. "Mr. Salisbury in town said he and Gilbert McCrery stole his service revolver from his saloon. Then they ran off. I'd like to bring in your boy for questioning." Roger Townsend looked to the back of his home. His son lay in bed like a corpse. He would've preferred to die right there than be dragged out of his house in shame.

"Boy!" His father shouted. A tear bloomed in the corner of his eye. "Boy!" His father hollered again. He didn't stir. "Boy!" The death knell of his father's voice finally brought him to his feet. He wouldn't hurt his father any longer by forcing him to retrieve his son for his arrest. Harris Townsend walked into the arms of justice without another word or struggle.

At the trial, Mr. Salisbury revealed that he had not served as an officer for the Union during the war, but he'd never said he had. The reputation of his establishment was unchanged by that confession. He managed to scrape by after the story died down.

Gilbert McCrery confessed to his crimes. The judge charged him with being an accessory to the theft of the revolver and the murder of that little girl. He wouldn't be hanged. He was simply tried for the crime of not standing up to his friend when he was wrong. A crime, I admit, that seems easy to commit. He was sent to a prison in Kansas City for fifteen years with a penalty. If he ever stepped foot in Chugwater Bluff of the Wyoming Territory again, he would be hanged.

That left Harris Townsend in front of the court. The town had gathered in the church to see the punishment be declared. The crowd didn't care about Mr. Salisbury's confession or Gilbert McCrery's crime of cowardice. They were only there to see Harris Townsend be brought to justice.

"Murderer!" The women cried. The men's fists curled in anger. Their words weren't permitted in a church. An appointed lawyer joined Harris Townsend at the stand.

"Prejudice will not be heard in this courtroom!" The judge shouted. The room went silent, quicker than the judge had expected. "Young man, you have been brought to this court to be tried for the crimes of involuntary murder and theft of a firearm. How do you plead?" Chugwater Bluff was silent for the first time in days, waiting for his answer.

"Guilty, your honor." It was as simple as that. The crowd's righteous anger was reduced to silence. They already had their wicked criminal in chains. He didn't even put up a fight. The boy who tasted his first whiskey that night became a man in the most horrible way. His negligence was made clear to all of those who lived near Chugwater Bluff. They were repeated for my private horror at his execution.

On the day of the hanging, after the gallows had been built by my worn hands, the marshal dragged Harris Townsend through the street in chains. Harris was always one step behind him. He tried to act tough, as if the sting of death wasn't anything to be fearful of. He climbed the steps of the gallows without help from neither the marshal's hand nor mine. I guided him to the spot. The marshal asked for his last words. He shuddered. I was behind him, so I couldn't see his tears, but he shook at the shoulders and bowed his head low.

"I'm sorry for what I did," he sobbed. He looked out at the people of Chugwater Bluff with submerged eyes. "I'm sorry for what I did. I didn't... I tried not..." He stuttered and moaned. I looked to the marshal, and he pushed his elbow out, telling me to go on. I put the sack over the boy's head, and he gasped his last gasp. I stepped to the lever in an instant. The marshal wanted to have the pleasure of counting down, but I saw it in his eyes before he could do it. I threw the lever back and let the boy hang.

Those women shouting about temperance when I was a boy came back to my memory. Most of the trouble that came with drinking was reserved for men. The fist fights or foul language was between men, never children. I didn't realize how foolish I had been to ignore their warnings and lamentations. It made me stick to well water for almost a year.

He was certainly the youngest man I hanged. He was a little smaller than I had expected. He was too young to die but too careless to leave unpunished. The problem is that the world is always sober. No matter how many times it sees the sun or how many barrels of beer it has to offer, it's always the same. No matter how you want to feel after drinking, you don't get to run out on the consequences. You can still be tried. You can still be hanged. You can hurt those around you when you don't have a care in the world. A man is supposed to be reliable for those in need, and Harris Townsend was no man. He died in the center of Chugwater Bluff for a little taste of whiskey.

## *The Hanging in a Town Called Hooker*

To call Hooker a ghost town would be wrong, but it's an honest mistake. Hooker was never more than an outpost on the path to Cheyenne. Cowboys would bring their day to an end in Hooker before getting paid in Cheyenne. The drinks were cheap and the women were too. Hooker, named after the general, was inhabited by a breed of women of the same name. The town was made of two buildings, the brothel and a halfway house. There was one other building outside of Hooker that didn't seem to fit in. It was a church made of canvas.

Father McGee was a young priest from Baltimore. He was sent out west for unspoken reasons, and he decided to bring his church to Hooker. The Wyoming Territory, despite its large population of Christians, needed to be evangelized, and there was no better place to start than the town of Hooker.

Sundays were very strange days in that town. Father McGee would deliver his sermon to a handful of the women. The big tent church existed in harmony with the town or, at least, took no notice in how the town conducted itself six days out of the seven.

On one Sunday, a few days before I was called to town, a mousy, young woman sat at a pew in silence. The service had finished, and the dirt remained settled on the ground since the last Sunday, except for where she sat and tread. Father McGee cleaned the chalice before looking to the young woman. Her dress had a large bow on the back and several laces covering her breast. Her hands were folded and her eyes downcast. The priest's toes tapped across the dirt floor.

"Magdalena, can I help you?" He asked. She stood; her eyes hardly lifted. They did not meet the pale gray eyes of the priest. His gaped mouth clamped shut as she lifted the sheet and disappeared behind it.

She marched with her toes out and her head down, past the well and halfway house before she passed through the saloon doors of the brothel. Nobody was downstairs. They had no customers the night before, and the bar was full of bottles without any men at the bar. The stairs groaned as she ascended and each room on the second floor held a slumbering woman. Their slight snores and breaths hummed out into the hall.

Magdalena sat in front of a mirror, unbundling the curls from the top of her head. In the light of the rising sun, her visage was clear to see. Her cheeks were pale and grew darker along her jaw. Her brown fingers wiped away the mascara from her eyes. She used to be strong. She used to hold her head high. Her fingernail traced the edge of her mirror as she looked into her own eyes. Clarity and solace could not be found. She looked elsewhere and searched the halls. She found another young woman and brought her to her room.

"Magdalena, what are you doing?" The young woman asked.

"I need help, Ruby. Please, just help me," Magdalena implored.

"What is it? The fellas are going to be here any minute," Ruby said.

"I want to know if… I want to know…"

"What is it?" Ruby snapped.

"Have you ever had any doubt about what you were doing was right?" There was silence. Ruby looked like her mind was fishing for answers.

"What are you talking about now, Magdalena?"

"I don't know what I'm doing anymore, and I don't know why." She ran to the bed and covered her face. Soft sobs pressed against her frail hands. Ruby walked to the side of the bed and held Magdalena's hand.

"It can't be as bad as it seems, sweetheart," Ruby cooed.

"But it is. I only believe in heaven because it can't get any worse than this. There has to be something better someday. And if I believe in heaven, how can I do what I've done?"

"You just got to do it because you got to do something. I'm not sure what you're talking about." Magdalena sat up and looked her friend in the eyes.

"I can't do this anymore, Ruby. I can't work like this."

"What're you going to do then? There's nothing else around to do."

"I'll leave. I'll go to Cheyenne and find a job there."

"What kind of job?"

"I don't know, but I can find something."

"Well...wait a minute. Can you even read?" Magdalena slapped Ruby's face. Ruby gasped and rubbed her cheek.

"I'm sorry, Ruby, you know how cross I can get." She rubbed her friend's hand and smiled.

"Now that you've roughed me up, do you feel better?" Ruby giggled. Magdalena's grin grew.

"No, but I'm glad I'm not alone in this place." Ruby's hand wrapped around Magdalena's wrist. Her tiny thumb rose and fell over the crook between Magdalena's hand and forearm.

"I should get ready for the boys. They'll be coming soon." Ruby stood and floated off to her room. Magdalena was left alone, alone with her conscience. She dug her nails into the bed. She felt repulsed. A jolt ran from her hands to her shoulders. Disgust was all she could feel.

"One more night," she told herself. "You can't afford not to work tonight," she realized. She stayed in her boudoir until a knock shook the room. A slobbering drunkard entered, and she hid under the covers. That just made him more interested. He wiped his nose and mouth. His stench filled the room. His weight shifted to one foot and then the other. His huge frame fell on the bed. Then she could feel him, with his fat fingers constricting around her.

In the morning, the town was quiet, and Magdalena went out to the well with a few pails in hand. She pulled at the straining rope to feel the bucket's weight. She wrapped some around her shoulders and started to elevate the bucket to the top. The black water ebbed as the bucket left the bottom of the well, growing paler as it reached the surface. When it reached the top, Magdalena poured its contents into her pail. She took the rope away from her shoulders and slowly lowered it down, watching it descend into the dark pool.

Beyond the breeze, she heard a distant cry. A disturbance grew as she filled her last pail of water. Finally, the bellows and the groans drew her eyes to the horizon. Four horsemen were taking a herd of cattle towards her. In the front was a man on a brown and white horse. His strapping shoulders didn't ease. His determined form only shifted by sight in the heat. Magdalena knew this man. She hurried inside and left the pails on the top of the bar.

Magdalena's weeping forced Ruby to dart into her boudoir and stop the commotion. Seeing Ruby,

Magdalena hid under the covers, sobbing pathetically. Ruby stepped closer to the bed and stood over her friend's shivering form.

"I can't do it again," Magdalena managed to shake out. "He's back."

"Who's back?" Ruby asked.

"You damn well know who!" Her shaded eyes glared at Ruby. "He's going to hurt me. I can't do it again."

"How do you know it was him?"

"I saw him coming to town. They're downstairs. I can hear them. See for yourself if you don't believe me." Ruby left her to her weeping. She closed the door to a soft knock as the door moved into place. Her feet stroked the floor, and she crept to the edge of the stairs. Four cowboys were corralled around the bar.

"One more round, Mickey," the tallest one said. His mustache was square just like his head. Ruby stood at the end of the bar, not giving her usual sultry grin. Mickey poured them each another mug of beer and looked to Ruby.

"What're you standing around for?" Mickey snapped. "What do you want?" He said before licking the middle of his white mustache. Ruby paid no attention to Mickey and stared at the head of the cowboy crew.

"Howdy, partner," she said, leaning over the counter. The cowboy sipped from his mug, never glancing away.

"Howdy," he said. She extended her hand.

"Want to go upstairs?" She asked. He said nothing and followed her eyes to the second floor. The other women moved around Ruby and her client as the pair made their way to her room.

Magdalena stayed under the blankets of her bed, sweating, with hot tears parting her face. She heard the footsteps of the other girls, then a grunt from a man. She couldn't recognize him. The sheet flew, and she lowered herself to the floor. She pressed her nose against the wood, peering through the slit. She saw Mickey's baldhead or nothing at all. The shapes shifted and rearranged themselves. There was no sign of him.

Ruby lay on the bed and looked away from her client. He jostled his belt up his legs. He buckled his pants and opened the door. She didn't look. Her eyes were elsewhere, far away. He knew why. He looked across the hall. His brow rose. A smile cracked across his dry face. He took his shirt and strode to the next room. Ruby wasn't there to see him.

The door swung open like a smooth breeze had

turned the knob. He made a move to close it quickly and played with a button on his shirt. Magdalena rose from the floor. Her small feet dug into the wood at the sight of him.

"Don't come near me, Rhett!" Her muscles shuddered. Rhett licked his bottom lip and tipped his head back.

"Here," he stacked some coins on the armoire. "Now I have to come over there." She jumped onto the bed and reached the other side. He stood his ground. His smile grew and made her feel more trapped.

"Stay where you are. Go somewhere else."

"I don't want to go anywhere else. You're the one I've been looking for."

"Out!"

"I can take my time. Just like last time," he said. He wiped his nose and took a step forward. She backed into the corner.

"Oh," he said. He looked down at his belt. There was a revolver with several bullets resting along his waist. "Let me take this off." He slipped the belt off and handed it to the armoire.

"Don't," Magdalena begged.

"I don't want to hurt you too bad. Now give us a kiss, darling." His wet lips led first and his hands reached out. Magdalena forced a howl and dove across the bed, under his arms. She landed and her hands stretched out for the belt on the armoire. She whirled around and pointed the revolver at her tormentor. Its holster hung on the end. Rhett kept his hands at his sides.

"What're you doing, darling? You know I don't want to hurt you. Now put that down, so I don't have to." He stepped closer.

"No," she winced. He didn't stop. He stood two steps away from the revolver's barrel. "Don't take another step!" His foot fell against the floor.

Sparks flew out and knocked him on his back. His blood spilled from his chest like a tipped ink well. He held himself up on his elbow and looked at his wound. He wanted to touch it to make sure it was real, but his veins felt cold. Magdalena watched him die.

Mickey tried to stop the three cowboys from taking Magdalena away. He held his ground on the stairs and quarreled with them until they forced their way out. Hogtied and lost to shock, Magdalena was delivered to justice in Cheyenne.

The day of her execution was set a few days after they brought her to town. Nobody in the town of Hooker owned a horse, so there could be no witnesses to testify in her defense. The judge believed it was a robbery gone wrong; after all, she was a sinner. Who knew what else she was capable of? It's not as if whores were known for telling the truth. In her cell, before her death, she had one request. She wanted to be hanged in Hooker.

The dusty ghost town had a sign of life, even on that day of death. They came out of the brothel like prairie dogs from their holes and formed a line to watch Magdalena on her way. The only strangers in that town were the marshal and me. The marshal held her by the arm and marched her to the stairs. Father McGee looked into Magdalena's sorrowful eyes.

"Forgive me, father," she said. "I wanted to leave this place. I wanted to stop being who I am. Please forgive me for my sins." Tears leapt from her cheeks. Father McGee touched her shoulders and lowered his head towards hers.

"You are forgiven, my child; reject sin, and love our Lord. He will be with you always." He made the sign of the cross, and Magdalena did so with the hindrance of her chains before being pushed up the steps. The marshal handed her to me. Her eyes looked away. I placed her on the trap door.

"Any last words?" I asked. Father McGee looked up at Magdalena as the sunlight shone over her figure. Mickey, Ruby, and the other women of infamy stood, weeping in sorrow and watching in fascination.

"I wanted to change. I wish things were different. I know that cannot be. I love you all," she said. "God forgive me," she whispered. Her head hung low, and the tears bubbled under her eyes. I put the sack over her head. I stood at the ready. The marshal nodded to me.

My tongue shifted in my mouth. My palms grew pale and damp. I reached for the lever and leaned back, letting the pull of my weight do the job, rather than my willing hand. The women yelped and turned away. Father McGee looked on, despite finding the sight of her death unbearable. Mickey, with sunken eyes and rough, engorged hands, led the women back into the brothel, a parade of the sorriest mourners I ever saw. Then I saw Father McGee begin to take down his beloved tented church.

## *The Hanging of a Horse Thief*

Blue Comet was her name. She had been around. The night she was born, a lantern fell and caused a fire in the stable. The door of their pen was loose, which gave them their escape. Blue Comet and her mother flew out from their burning shelter and followed the ember-lit path into the darkness. Blue Comet, still a pony, was found alone by a circus headed out west.

She dipped her snout into a slow-running creek as the circus performers dragged everything they had across the plains. The maestro of the circus, Julius the Clown, suddenly had a glimmer in his eye. Finding that pony lifted his spirits like seeing the sun after days of rain. He jumped off his cart and crossed the creek. The pony paid no mind. She tipped her head up when she felt his meaty hand stroking her mane. When he knew that he had reassured the little creature, he hoisted her onto his shoulders and carried her back to the party of performers. She never twisted nor neighed. He smiled from ear to ear, thinking of how to use her in one of their acts.

Her first profession was to pull a pair of dwarves on a chariot in a race with other ponies. Blue Comet was a Lipizzaner, a beautiful white horse that was born to race.

Word spread that the owner of the stable was searching for his lost horses. When Julius the Clown heard this, he had an idea. His lip curled into a grin. He would have to disguise his new horse. Every mark of the animal that could be identified by the owner had to be covered.

Julius the Clown bought a pail of blue paint from the nearest general store and gave her a new coat. He gave her the name and painted her from head to hoof, except for one part. He painted around her eyes to make them look like stars, and thus Blue Comet was born.

Julius displayed his new, blue horse at the next show and the crowd loved her. The owner was in attendance that night; he examined every horse he could see, but he couldn't tell that she was his horse, and he walked out of the big top into the night, dashing the clown's fears.

When the circus traveled further west, the fewer people were there to watch them perform. The big top folded before they reached Oregon and left Julius with a choice to make. Running on debt, the circus clown decided to end the show in Cheyenne. Blue Comet was in her prime and as strong as a horse could be. She pulled carriages full of circus folk to their stops, and this made her muscles ripple and throb. The governor of the Wyoming Territory saw their show and demanded to see the horse backstage. He paid Julius handsomely for it. He was so proud of his new horse that he called for a parade to celebrate. He and the circus, along with the local marching band, strode down Main Street. Outside a saloon were two shaggy-looking young men, eyeing up the creature.

"That's a pretty horse," Clive told his brother.

"That she is," Daryl opined. "I wonder what a man has to do to get one of those."

"I heard that she's one of the last blue horses in the world."

"Really? That must make her very expensive then."

"I guess it's kind of like those stories about King Arthur, you know, about the horses with big horns on their heads." Clive chuckled.

"Is that what you want, brother? A unicorn?" Daryl said with a sly look in his eye.

"If I could get me one of those blue horses," Clive said, clutching his cap in his hands. "I'd be the happiest man alive. I wouldn't even do anything else. I'd just ride all day long and then sleep all night, dreaming about riding in the morning." Daryl leaned against the post that separated him from his brother and watched as the horse turned the corner.

"Maybe there's a way we can make that so, brother dear."

"You really think so?"

"Sure, I'm sure, let me think of something first." Daryl chewed on his lip and watched the circus performers dance their last dance and wave to their last crowd. They turned the corner, letting Daryl make his designs, out of sight.

After the festivities came to an end, Daryl and Clive returned to their room in a tenement house. Daryl counted the coins in his pocket and ran his hand across the bottom of a drawer, finding a few more dollars.

"Do you think that will be enough?" Clive asked. Daryl counted the coins again and tallied their expenses in his mind.

"I think it should be. We don't need to buy the horse. We just want to know where we can find another one." Daryl and Clive set out for the barbershop for a shave and a haircut to present themselves to the governor.

All perfumed and clean for the first time in months, they knocked on the governor's door. The door swung open with a butler behind it. His stern countenance did not shatter the hope expressed on their faces. The butler cleared his tight, cordy throat and adjusted his sweating collar.

"Can I help you, gentlemen?" He spoke from the cavern of his core.

"We'd like to seek audience with the governor," Clive said with a bow. Daryl looked at his brother with an incredulous expression and swung back to face the butler.

"We just want to ask him about his uh...just ask him some questions." Daryl cleared his throat and waited, hoping the butler would be forgiving. The silence between them wasn't one of patience or speechlessness but one of measured disdain.

"What do you wish to ask the governor?"

"Well we'd like to keep that to ourselves," Clive said. Daryl hit him in the arm.

"What my brother is trying to say is that we would like to speak to the governor ourselves rather than use you as a messenger." The butler didn't move a muscle. "It's about the horse, sir."

"The horse?" the butler asked.

"Yes, sir, it's the blue beauty that he rode into town." The butler steamed from the nose.

"The horse is not for sale, gentlemen. Good day," he said, trying to close the door. Daryl pressed his hand against it.

"We don't want to buy it. We just want to know where he got it." The butler pushed the door shut. Daryl didn't raise his hand again. Clive kicked his boot at the air.

"Let's go to the bar," Daryl grunted.

At the much-frequented Golden Pearl, Clive and Daryl shared a bottle of whiskey in the center of the room. Other workingmen and travelers sat back and listened to the fiddler play a tune.

"I'm sorry, Clive."

"It's alright. We did our best."

"That butler wasn't very nice to us. It wasn't right."

"No, it's alright. I don't mind not having a horse. I never had one to begin with." Clive twisted his cap in his hands. Daryl frowned and thumbed the top of his glass.

"There'll be other horses," Daryl offered. Clive didn't say anything. "Rich folks always want to keep things to themselves. We just wanted some information, not even that horse." Clive raised his sorry head. "Although we would have taken it, if they would have parted with it." Daryl poured himself another glass. Clive's glass was filled to the top. He didn't touch it, turning the cap in his hands.

"To hell with the rich!" Daryl raised his glass. Clive remained motionless. Daryl pushed his brother's glass forward. "Go on, to hell with the rich!"

"To hell with the rich," Clive mumbled along.

"To hell with the rich," Daryl murmured against his glass. After a satisfied groan, the glass clapped against the table.

"You shouldn't drink so much," Clive said. His eyes moved up to his glass. "You know how you get." Daryl poured another glass.

"We can't be liquored up," Clive implored. "We have to work in the morning." Now Clive looked his brother in the face. Daryl ignored his brother's concern and sipped more of his whiskey.

"All that money on cutting our hair, and for what?" Daryl groaned. Clive grinned a little and took his glass in hand.

"At least we look good, eh?" The brothers chuckled. They touched glasses and enjoyed the buzzing feeling in their legs. Then Daryl's face fell into a pensive state.

"They'll still never treat us right, brother. No matter what we do, they'll treat us like trash. That butler, the governor's servant, he treated you like you were an idiot."

"Maybe I am. I'm not the-"

"No." Daryl swung his fist down on the table and missed, hitting the edge with a small tap. "No, you're not trash. You're a good boy. You're my kid brother, and nobody treats you like that." Clive's smile jumped a bit.

"Thank you, brother," he said weakly. He sipped at his drink.

"Look at me," Daryl said. Clive did as he was told. "I'm going to get you that horse. One way or another." Clive tried to protest, but Daryl raised his hand and gave him his stern brotherly look.

"Just think of it as your Christmas present come early." Clive grinned again. Imagining the thought opened his smile wide.

"What would you do with a horse like that?" Daryl asked.

"Ride him as much as I can," Clive said with eyes a mile away.

"Or we could use him for racing. We could head over to Kentucky and win the derby." Daryl kept his eye on Clive until his brother recognized that that was the smarter plan. Clive did so and reclined in his seat.

"So, what're we going to do?"

"We're going to take it," Daryl said as he licked his lips. Clive sat up and hunched over the table with narrowed eyes.

"You know taking a governor's horse is stealing, right?" Daryl guffawed and let his head swirl as he leaned back in his chair. He looked up at the ceiling and imagined the stars beyond it.

"I want to give my brother a horse for a present. What do you say, Clive?" Clive looked around. Nobody was listening to what they had to say.

"She is a pretty horse," Clive admitted.

"And not just her, we'll each have one. We can do it," Daryl said.

"I like the sound of that."

"How about tonight?" Daryl asked. Clive looked away to ponder. He couldn't disappoint his brother, especially when Blue Comet was theirs for the taking.

"I'll do it."

"Excellent," Daryl said. He clapped and rubbed his hands. Their plan was the most exciting thing to have happened in that saloon, and it was happening underneath everybody's noses.

"I do have one question though," Clive said with a raised finger.

"Yes, brother," Daryl said in a delighted tone.

"Let's say we sneak past everyone and go to the governor's stables, how are we going to get away with it?"

"We'll split up," Daryl planned. "You'll go to Salt Lake City, and I'll go to Imperial. When they've given up, we'll meet up again. We'll meet in Denver City on Christmas."

"I don't want to be away from you for that long."

"We have to get away for a long enough time for them to give up. We'll see each other again. Once Christmas comes around, we can make a whole new life. We don't need to work for anybody anymore once we have that blue beauty underneath you." Daryl and Clive finished their bottle of whiskey as the sun melted against the horizon.

At their tenement, Daryl lit a candle and watched it stand in its brass holder. His eyes did not stray, and his thoughts turned to pensive brooding.

"Tonight it is," he told Clive. "I can feel it in my bones. I almost never feel this strongly about anything, but I do now. Tonight is the night. I hope you're not tired, brother. We have work to do." Clive watched his brother with troubled eyes.

"You sound...well you seem different tonight."

"This is it; I tell you. As sure as this flame burns, this is the night we do it."

"But," Clive muttered. Daryl flew around with piercing, negotiating eyes.

"We can't say that now. We need all of the strength we have for this." He sighed with a smile at the flame. "There's only one path left. Are you ready, Clive?" Daryl didn't hear a response for several moments. Clive, watching his brother, had to make up his mind. He had to make up his mind to make up his mind in the first place. He thought deeply. As his inspired brother turned his head, he knew what to do, so as not to disappoint his brother but also stir strength within himself.

"I'm ready, Daryl." Daryl grinned and then looked back at the flame.

"One more hour, and then we'll go." After continuing his stare at the candle, he eventually slunk back into his corner of the room, sat on the bed, and disappeared into the darkness.

The darkness of the night stayed as the clouds held their stead below the moon. Daryl and Clive walked off the path from town and traversed through the woods behind the governor's home to find the stables. Their lantern light could be seen for half a mile, if anyone was awake to see them. Crouched in the thorny underbrush, Daryl and Clive made the last decisions of their plan.

"There it is. The home of the best horses in the territory," Daryl said. His teeth glowed in the light. He patted his brother on the back, and Clive's eyes grew brighter as he realized his brother's words were true.

"So, what do we do now?" Clive asked.

"We will have to move very quietly," Daryl

whispered. He began to crawl through the shrubs, and his brother followed. When they came from underneath the brush, they started to tiptoe towards the stable. Clive started to giggle as they walked closer. Daryl tried to silence his brother with a hiss. Soon, they both couldn't help it. They were naughty boys trying to steal a chicken. It was just a childhood game to them.

When they reached the far wall of the stable, they could hear the animals breathing in deep sleep. Daryl put his finger to his lips and pointed to the side of the stable. They crept around the corner, hoping they wouldn't awaken the snoring governor or his servants.

Clive pulled the stable door to the side. In that stable were a dozen of the finest thoroughbred creatures a man could find. They were strong, bold, and a work of art in the light of a lantern. The horses woke from their slumber as Clive and Daryl looked at each one. Then came a tall creature with skin as blue as the sky. They were stunned, caught off guard by the beautiful face staring back at them, surrounded by darkness.

After finding Blue Comet in her shining color, Daryl and Clive opened her pen and placed the saddle on her back. The horse began to shuffle its hooves and neighed as Clive squirmed on its back.

"Quiet, girl," Clive said with a delicate press of his hand.

"I'm going to take these two," Daryl whispered. Clive stepped down.

"Let me help," he said. Daryl's apprehension flashed across his face, but he hid it for his brother's helping hand. When the gates were opened for Daryl's coveted creatures, they started to gurgle and whine. Daryl took their reins and pulled them ahead. One bucked back and hissed. Its legs hit the side of the stable. Clive pulled Blue Comet closer to the door, away from the frustrated black beauties. They wouldn't stop roaring and writhing.

A call came from the house. Clive, gob smacked, looked at the governor's windows. A light began to bloom inside the house. He wanted to warn his brother but making a sound might foil their scheme.

"Quiet down," Daryl demanded. The horses kicked and cried, no matter how hard he pulled. Clive looked back to the window and saw a light flicker towards the rear door.

"Daryl, someone's on to us." Daryl looked at the window and saw the light move through the house.

"Go," Daryl whispered fiercely. "Due west and don't stop 'til you get to Salt Lake." Clive hopped onto Blue Comet and kicked her hind legs. She ran off and Clive almost lost his head as she raced out of the stable. His lantern led the way.

"Hey you! Get back here, you son of a bitch!" The man from the house shouted. Daryl kept pulling at the horses. He held the reins in one hand and the lantern in the other. The lantern's light caught the eye of the governor's servant. The horses dragged their hooves, picking up straw along the stable floor.

"If there's another one of you, you can forget taking anymore horses! Come on out of there! No foolishness now!" Daryl kept pulling. His lantern floated in his shaking hand. The servant aimed his weapon at the stables. The loud noise of gunfire was accompanied by the cracking of wood. All of the horses reared in their pens and screamed so that the stars could hear.

"This next bullet has your name on it, boy!" The servant gritted his teeth and stepped closer. Daryl was on one knee, holding the reins. His mind flashed from the windows of the stable to the door. Quick, he thought, make up your mind. He spread himself out along the wall and struck the horses on their rears. They shot out of the stable like they were on fire. The servant saw them run and fired above them, hoping to strike the thief. He didn't see anything fall from the horses' back, so he rammed his hand down his pocket to reload his shotgun.

"It's over!" He shouted as he ran to the stable door. "Put your hands up!" He snapped the barrel closed and turned the corner. All Daryl had left was the lantern in his hand and horse apples at his feet. He surrendered peacefully.

At the courthouse, the judge made short work of Daryl. The governor, horribly mistreated, insisted on a speedy trial, one with a guilty verdict. He even decided to see the horse thief tried. The judge looked Daryl up and down as soon as he was brought in wearing chains around his ankles.

"I have two simple questions," the judge said. "There is no way out of this for you. The punishment for this crime can be reduced if you answer these questions to the court's pleasure. Are you willing to comply?"

"I might," Daryl said, much to his lawyer's embarrassment.

"Well you better, for your sake," the judge said. Daryl rolled his shoulders and waited patiently. "Who stole the governor's horse?" Daryl said nothing. The judge asked again. Daryl held his tongue.

"Answer the judge," Daryl's lawyer whispered to him.

"Where did he go?" The judge asked him.

"He left the territory, and I won't ever tell you where!" Daryl roared, shaking his manacles. His lawyer placed his head in his hands. The judge rested back in his sit, reckoning the cost for defiance.

"You leave me with no choice," the judge said. "I will convene in my quarters to prescribe the proper punishment for your crimes. You have done yourself no favors." The judge stood and the rest of the court's audience joined him as he left.

Of course, Daryl was sentenced to death. For not betraying his brother, he was to be executed. Death is a serious toll. It shouldn't be dealt with in such a capricious manner. I never liked that case. I didn't care about the money. There were all kinds of violent scoundrels across the territory that deserved it more than that horse thief. The judge and that governor wanted to make an example out of him. I didn't for a moment want to make him one.

## The Hanging of a Prospector

After my start as a hangman, I thought back on the guilty, a boy, a wronged woman, and a devoted brother. All had done wrong, but I never felt sure of myself. I never thought of them as an evil that had to be rid of. Even Harris Townsend was repentant. His stinging tears made me feel lost on the gallows, but I was reminded of the blood he shed, and then I thought of Rock Springs.

The coal country of the Wyoming Territory was known for its lowlifes and corruption. It only took one visit to understand why. The city of Rock Springs, if you can call it that, supported coal miners, prostitutes, and their bastards. It had a reputation that had spread across the plains. Even in New York, it only came to their minds as Sodom and Gomorrah, which, I've been told, is saying something. I was called to Rock Springs for a hanging. I remember that the smell there was unnatural, despite it surely coming from the earth.

Rock Springs was nothing but grit. It looked like a million chunks of coal had been turned to powder and had fallen on the town like snow. Seeing the dark grime on the houses and shacks made me want to stay on the train. I took a step onto the platform. The moment I had, the miners who were unoccupied glared at me. Their black cheeks and yellow eyes made me think I had crossed the river Styx. It seemed like I had passed through the world, into a darker place with no way to return.

When I started to build the scaffold, I noticed my hands had become as dark as oil. The ground was stained with a darkness that couldn't be brushed away. They couldn't grow a plant in that town if they tried. My black prints were left all over the white wood of the gallows and, after hearing the man's story, I understood why I couldn't just wash the slate clean.

The tavern, called the Broken Spade, was made of thick tree trunks stacked on top of each other. The old, weathered miners held mugs in their hands and mumbled about any news they had to share. A round-faced, slovenly young man at the bar was slurping his soup and washing it down with a mug of beer. When he spilt, he rubbed his coal-colored hands across his unshaved jaw. The barman kept his eye on him for a moment and then surveyed the rest of the tavern before returning his gaze to him. The wide door swung open, revealing an old man with a head of hair and a beard of snow. He walked towards the young man and took his shoulder.

"Luke," he said.

The young man wiped the stubble on his cheek and looked at him.

"I found it," the old man said.

"What did you find?" Luke asked like a simpleton.

"It's the big one," the old man whispered.

"Pa, what are you talking about?" Luke asked.

"I've found enough gold to fill that mug," he said.

"Where is it? Do you have it?" Luke asked, and his father shushed him. Luke looked to see if anyone had noticed, but his father turned him back to the bar.

"It's up at Putnam Peak," the old man whispered into his son's ear. "It took me all day to climb it, but I found it in a cave. It's twice the size of your head. I need your help. You can climb as well as anyone, and I'll show you the spot. That way we can take it all in one go, straight to the bank. You'll help me, won't you?"

"I won't let you down, Pa." They shared a smile the size of a canoe.

Soon after this familial exchange, the wide door opened again. Some of the patrons groaned at the white light as a man stood there, his shoulders back. He closed the door and marched to the bar. He corralled Luke's father around the shoulders.

"How are you doing, Bobby?" the man asked.

"Hey there, Walsh," Bobby said. "How was the digging at Golden Rock?"

"Well," Walsh said, as he took off his hat. "I tried but no luck." He knocked his fist on the bar.

"I'm sorry to hear that. What're you going to do now?" Bobby asked. Walsh got a funny look in his eye. He let out a laugh that filled the room, and his eyes grew as they stared at Bobby's bearded face.

"That's why I came to see you. I thought that I could rely on my old friend to help me find some work. At least for a little while," he said. He took a seat on the stool and tapped his palm on the bar.

"Oh, well what did you have in mind?"

"I'm not sure. I was wondering what kind of work there may be in town here." Walsh locked eyes with the barman. "A whiskey, friend." The barman procured one right away.

"Well you know that I don't work at the mine anymore," Bobby said.

"That I do know. What have you been up to since?" Walsh said with the glass in his hand.

"I've been prospecting myself. After that last cave in, you know my body hasn't been the same. The lungs burn easy, and my legs get weak," Bobby assured him. Walsh waited for him to continue. "So that's why I'm out of the mines and looking elsewhere for my two bits." Walsh drank and wiped his lips with the back of his hand, revealing a smile. He leaned in closer.

"Where do you go looking then?"

"I can't really say."

"You've found something then?" Walsh's eyes grew larger, like a wolf at a slaughtered deer.

"I don't want to let other folks know. My boy and I are going to look tomorrow to make sure that we have something." Walsh drank from his glass, keeping his eyes on Bobby.

"I bet you could use another hand to help you out." Bobby gulped and stammered. Walsh shook his head a bit with the same grin. "You don't want to share any, do you?"

"It's ours, Walsh," Bobby implored. "I found it. It's…"

"So you wouldn't want anyone to know?" Walsh boomed. Bobby touched his arm to keep him quiet. He bared his teeth slightly, not to frighten Walsh, but out of desperation. His scared eyes retreated when Walsh looked at his hand on his arm.

"Please, Walsh, not here," Bobby begged. Walsh's breath steamed from his nose.

"How many years were we in the mines together?" Walsh growled.

"Every year, Walsh, I remember."

"And you can't help your friend, your friend who has known you for so long to find some little bit of relief from all the searching after we retired?" Luke had never taken his eyes off of Walsh since he approached his father.

"All right, Walsh, we'll all go together. It'll be all right. Just don't tell anyone," Bobby insisted. Walsh bared his teeth and laughed. Seeing his father being pushed around didn't make Luke feel ashamed of him; he felt just as frightened as he did.

"I'll see you here," he pointed at the bar. "Tomorrow at ten o'clock. It'll be like old times." Walsh patted a stiff Bobby on the shoulder. Luke and his father watched as Walsh left the tavern, the door crashing behind him. After taking a moment to collect his thoughts, Bobby turned to his son.

"You can't tell anyone about this," Bobby whispered. "Three's a crowd already. We can't let anybody else know." Luke didn't answer. He simply stared at his father in shock.

"Say something, boy," Bobby rattled him. Luke looked past his father, making sure Walsh was truly gone. The tension in his shoulders loosened.

"Yes, Pa," he said.

"Good, I will see you later at the house." Bobby shuffled off to the door. Luke asked for another drink and sipped it, thinking to himself. He looked around the tavern. Most of the miners were grumbling to each other and slurping at their mugs. Luke found a familiar pair at a table near the wall. He lowered himself from the stool and reached them in no time at all.

"Fellas, I have to tell you something," Luke said. The pair looked up, taken aback.

"What is it, Luke?" One of them said.

"I'm going out tomorrow with my pa to Putnam

Peak. There's that fella you just saw coming with us. I just want you to know that. Now I need to go."

"Wait, Luke, what's going on?" The same one asked. Luke was already halfway to the door. "Do you know what he's talking about?"

"They're going to Putnam Peak tomorrow," the other said while pressing tobacco into his pipe.

"What for?" His friend lit a match and puffed on his pipe in thought.

"It's his day off. He can do as he pleases." He wrapped his mouth around the pipe and puffed a few clouds of smoke. "You should steer clear of other people's business, Eli." Eli thought hard on what Luke had told them. He tapped his thumb on the table, and, like a stiff breeze, he realized his friend's intent.

"I got it. I... I think I... I should go." He stood up from the table and left his friend enjoying his pipe.

Luke swung open the door of the gunsmith and placed himself in front of the owner. The gunsmith curled his well-kept mustache and waited patiently for Luke to collect his words. He was catching his breath.

"I need a pistol. Something small," Luke said.

"You're not looking for a derringer, are you?" The gunsmith asked.

"No, but...well, maybe something a little bigger than that. Something that can stop a man in his tracks."

"A bullet flies faster than you can blink, sonny. Any gun can stop a man. What kind do you need?"

"A small pistol that I can hide will be fine. It's for protection."

"Just for protection?" the gunsmith asked with a raised eyebrow.

"Yes, it's for my father." The gunsmith shifted to his side, keeping his raised eye on Luke's sorry face.

"Why couldn't he come down here then?"

"He doesn't know he's in danger." The gunsmith licked his teeth, mulling over the veracity of his words.

"All right, I can give you a .22 revolver for ten dollars. Do you have the cash?" Luke's mouth went dry, and a shock went to his spine. He didn't have the money. He muttered something under his breath, and he walked headlong for the door. He didn't notice that Eli was walking into the store as he was leaving. Eli approached the counter and placed his hands on the top of it, at ease.

"How much for a small revolver?"

"Ten dollars," the gunsmith stated.

"Could I get it for eight?" Eli asked. The gunsmith glared. "Nine?" The gunsmith crossed his arms.

"You can have it for nine," he said.

Eli smiled and slapped the counter. He dug into his pocket and handed over the cash in full. The gunsmith took a small revolver from the wall behind him and placed it in front of Eli. Before Eli could take it, the gunsmith pulled it back across the counter.

"Do you want any bullets?" The gunsmith asked with glass eyes. Eli gulped and nodded. He tossed a dime on the table and received a box of bullets.

The pale sunlight pierced the holes of Luke and Bobby's home. It was a simple hut, perched up on the side of a hill not far from town. Bobby remembered a flood the first year the town was established, and he'd decided to make his home invincible to another. Luke thought of his father's folly as he looked through one of the small holes in the roof.

His father had just risen and was preparing his bag for the journey. Luke put his hands behind his head. He tried to see the meaning in the sunlight. It was a new day but an important day. They were about to find enough gold to make them governors, maybe even president. Could he tell that this day was special from the sun? Could he feel more powerful or refreshed with this knowledge on that morning? He could only feel it in his heart with inexorable determination. He hated that town. There had to have been a better life—one that had been out of his grasp, until that morning.

His father's clumsiness led to pots and pans clattering to the floor. Luke rose from his cot and helped his father pick up his mess. Bobby took the pan from Luke's hands and placed it on the counter with the rest of the accouterments.

"It's going to be a good day, son," Bobby said, looking at a pan and some eggs on a shelf. He cracked them onto the pan.

"After breakfast, I think we should go straight there. We don't need to wait around for Walsh," Luke said. Bobby lit a match to start the stove. He whisked it away and turned to his son.

"Luke, he's a good friend. We had to leave coal mining and prospect on our own. He doesn't have anything. Neither of us can stop working; we have nothing. I want to rest before my day comes, and I'll help him the best I can." Stunned by his father's words, Luke said nothing. Bobby returned his gaze to the cooking eggs. Luke thought in the silence. Should he speak out or be a dutiful son? What was his duty?

"I think he wants to take it all for himself, Pa," Luke said. Bobby's head turned like it weighed a ton. His eyes stood as straight as an arrow at Luke.

"You have a narrow mind, boy. There's only one way to look at things for you, isn't that right?"

"Pa, I know he helped you then, but that doesn't mean he'll help you now."

"You're dumber than a stack of bricks. What I say goes."

"I'm going to kill him, Pa. I'll cut him down as soon as he starts looking for trouble." Luke's body started to shake.

"You're not coming with us then. I don't need any trouble from you, and you can just head back to the mines for the rest of your money."

"Is he going to carry you up the peak, Pa? Two old men climbing Putnam Peak, just like one of your fairytales, huh?" A slap cracked across Luke's face. Luke's fists clenched and held at his side. He waited for another, and his father looked to his eggs.

"You're going to do as I tell you, Luke. I won't say it again." Luke stood still, like a good boy. A tear from Bobby's eye sizzled in the pan.

A minute before ten o'clock, Bobby and Luke took a seat at the bar. They had their gear for the journey sitting at their feet. They would be back by sunset, if not earlier. They had found it; they only needed to find it again. When the clock struck ten, Walsh thrust himself through the door. He smiled like his teeth were piano ivories.

"Good morning, Bobby, are you and your boy ready for destiny?" Walsh asked. Luke stared, and Bobby grinned the best he could.

"Of course, are you all set?" Bobby replied.

"Yes, I am. Let's have a drink." Walsh gave the barman a signal and three shots of whiskey appeared on the table. Luke's eyes hung low as they drank. He tapped his side to find the knife he'd brought. It was there, ready. He hoped he would be quick enough.

Putnam Peak was not too far from Rock Springs. It was a tall hill with boulders on top of boulders and a spire driving into the sky. Luke caught Walsh's smile as he looked behind him. There wasn't anyone following them on the trail. That didn't ease Luke's mind.

At the base, Bobby's hands started to shake as he prepared for his ascent. Luke helped his father touch the rock wall. Bobby gripped the first rock and pushed himself up. Luke waited for his father to climb high enough. He glanced at Walsh before ascending. Walsh gave him a wry grin.

Bobby groaned as the rocks scratched at his gut. That was the worst point, the point of no return. Luke and Walsh waited patiently for him to climb onward. The sweat grew on his palms, and a cold touch held in the back of his throat. He had to act.

"Pa, do you need some help?" Luke asked. Bobby reached further and wiped the pools of sweat from his hand. He gritted his teeth and grunted to the next foothold. Bobby's strength was waning, but he couldn't let his son down. I made it up yesterday, why not today, he wondered. Luke saw him struggling and climbed faster to his side.

"Don't worry, Pa, I can help you," Luke offered his arm. Bobby's muscles started to wobble. He couldn't. He had to take his son's hand. Bobby leaned on his son like a feather. Luke used all his strength to pull them both up. He could feel their sweating hands start to separate. Hold on, Luke thought. His father grabbed the nearest rock that jutted out.

"Okay, son, I can take it from here," Bobby said. Luke hesitated to unhand him. Bobby reached up and took the next rock, but he lost his footing. His leg, floating away from the wall, felt like a ton of bricks. He tried to pull it back, but he couldn't find a landing. His hands slipped.

"Boy, I'm sorry," Bobby said. Exhaustion shone through his eyes. Luke's heart grew cold, to see his father so defeated. Bobby's arms shook like tremors.

"Climb on my back!" Luke cried.

"I can't. It'll kill us both."

"You have to do it, Pa. Do it!" Bobby knew he only had so much strength left to hold onto that rock. He extended his hand, and Luke lowered his shoulder. Bobby leaned onto his boy, holding him like a child to his mother.

Luke's muscles convulsed with the added weight. He was strong; he could tell his father had lost weight in the wilderness. His cage of bones didn't stop his son from reaching for the next rock. One slip of the hand, and they'd both be done for.

Walsh watched in awe. He had trouble during the climb, but he never knew Luke could do something like that. He'd never heard of any man doing that before.

The three prospectors heaved air into their lungs

once they were safe from the edge. Walsh looked at Luke like he had performed a miracle. Luke might have thought he had too, but he was only glad to have held on for as long as he had. It took all his strength, in every joint and sinew. Luke liked the look of shock in Walsh's eye, but Walsh's expression of amazement wasn't out of reverence. He was afraid, too.

"I thought you had climbed this rock before?" Walsh asked Bobby.

"It was just as difficult yesterday. Almost," Bobby chuckled, patting Luke's shoulder.

"How much longer do we have left?" Walsh asked.

"This is it," Bobby panted. "It's right around the corner. There's no need to hurry. We can wait for a bit."

"Where did you learn to climb like that?" Walsh asked Luke.

"Pa taught me. I got strong working in the mine." Walsh pondered what kind of labor would produce such strength. Whatever it was, he couldn't do it at his age. When the breathing got easier, the men stood and approached the corner of the peak.

"Now," Bobby started, catching his breath. "If you slip, try to reach for a branch, not one of us."

There was a large tree that grew up right next to the peak. Its nearest branch was five feet away.

"Stay close to the rocks," Bobby instructed. He kept his chest over the slope of the rocky hill and inched his way around the corner. Luke and Walsh watched him and followed, placing their feet where he had. As Walsh began to pull himself across, he heard a cry from above. He looked at the top of the peak. It was a small goat, crying out from the top of the world.

Bobby, having done this once before, was farther ahead of his son and Walsh. Luke dug his hands into the wall and lightly stepped closer to the corner where his father stood. His breath flew back in his face as his nose stayed close to the rocks. He didn't dare look down, as his foot slid towards the edge.

"Look out," Walsh grunted. He grabbed Luke's arm as he found his balance. Bobby looked back and saw that they had stopped.

"Are you all right over there?" Walsh gave Luke a hard stare and let go of him. Luke then stepped cautiously onward. Walsh looked up and his face expressed pure horror. Out of the blue expanse came rocks, silently falling down the side of the peak. Walsh let out a huge scream, and he jumped out and into the tree. The first branch snapped, but he landed on a sturdier one beneath it. The rocks crashed through the ends of the branches, clattering against the stones along the hill.

"Walsh!" Bobby shouted. Walsh held onto the wobbling tree. He was below the cliff and out of Luke's reach. It swayed as the wind gusted through. Luke kept his eyes on Walsh while digging his fingers into the rock. He wanted to leave, but he stayed. Perhaps it was out of fear, or duty to Walsh for helping him back up, but Luke stayed put. Walsh's wild eyes searched for a way back.

"Boy," Walsh said with an outstretched hand. "Help me." Luke seemed dumbfounded. Walsh grew irritated, tired of that slack-jawed look on his face.

"Help me!" He hollered. Luke looked down and saw the small margins behind his heels on the edge. He looked up and carefully turned to face Walsh. Every step, every sway seemed like it would be enough to topple him. Luke fixed his eyes on Walsh's hand.

"Now what?" Luke asked. "How are you going to get over here? I can't pull you in."

"Yes, you can! If you could climb with your pa on your back, you can give me a hand. Now do it!" Walsh was losing his grip. His elbows and chin were hanging above the branch he clung to. Luke took a peg from his bag and chiseled it into the wall. He took hold of it and leaned out to Walsh. Walsh shifted down the branch. It waned as he reached the edge.

"Give me your hand!" Walsh cried. Their fingers met, and Walsh took the leap of faith. Luke's hand slipped to the edge of the peg. Walsh's weight nearly took them over the edge. Luke's grasp tightened around Walsh's wrist, and he leaned back, bringing Walsh closer to the ledge. Walsh lifted himself from his elbow. Luke moved to the side, and Walsh reached for the peg up above to bring him to his feet. Luke didn't look back as he made it safely to his father.

Walsh, heaving and enraged, found father and son as they stood, mouth agape, at the alcove where they saw the gold. It was a deep cut of shining splendor. Luke had never seen gold before. A glittering river ran across the cavern, nearly the length of a man.

"Ain't she beautiful?" Bobby asked. Luke smiled like a little boy. Then he heard a snap. He turned around. Walsh's revolver was locked on his head. He grew as stiff as a board.

"You boys better start digging," Walsh commanded. Luke's brow shivered. When he'd lain in bed that morning, he didn't think it would be like that. He lowered his hand to his side, where the knife was waiting.

"Why, Walsh," Bobby asked. "Why would you do this?"

"I'm not waiting through another sleepless night in the rain. I'm not climbing; I'm not digging; I'm not working anymore either. I've done my working, and now it's time for me to get what's mine."

"I found this, Walsh. It doesn't belong to you." Luke stepped between Walsh and his father. Walsh's eyes cut between him and the gold.

"Out of the way, boy." Luke held a scowl on his face. His hand reached at his hip for the knife. He had one chance. "I said out of the way, boy." Luke's hand loosened the knife from his belt by half an inch. One pull from the belt and a push into the man's heart was all Luke needed.

Walsh fired a bullet, and it ricocheted off the gold. A spark flew from the cavern wall. Luke and Bobby ducked, and then Luke lunged forward. A bullet cracked and struck Luke in his very center. He collapsed, scraping the knife against Walsh's arm. Walsh winced and looked down at Luke, holding onto life while facing the rock floor of the alcove.

"You son of a bitch!" Bobby roared. He leapt on

top of Walsh and dragged him down. Walsh, on his side, reached for the revolver's hammer. Bobby clenched Walsh's wrist and struck him across the face with his right hand.

"You killed my boy!" Another blow struck down on Walsh's cheek. Walsh took Bobby by the throat and tried to wrench his arm free. Bobby leaned into Walsh's grasp to reach his face. Bobby's thumb dug into the side of Walsh's eye, gasping and reveling in his pain. Walsh's thumb pulled at the hammer as he roared in agony. His elbow bucked and struck Bobby's hand away from his face. His free hand stripped away Bobby's last chance of vengeance. The end of the revolver burned a hole in Bobby's neck. He groaned, wheezed, and choked, as his windpipe lay sideways in his throat. Walsh, disgusted, pushed Bobby's decaying form off of him.

Walsh picked himself up and took Bobby's pickaxe from his bag. He started to swing away. Chunks of it fell to the floor. Rocks of pure gold crashed at his feet. They were his for the taking. He laughed as his filled his bag with as much gold as he could carry. The bag weighed like an anchor at his side when he finished his task. He took it all. The greed and excitement flooded his senses. Looking from the top of Putnam Peak, the beautiful countryside seemed to open up to him. Its clouds started to run, revealing the bluest sky.

Walsh slowly lowered himself to the bottom of the peak. He lowered the gold to the ground and pulled as much air into his lungs as he could. Climbing down was always the trickiest part of it all. When he rose, he heard a rustle from a nearby tree. Eli strode forth with a determined brow. He pressed his small revolver into Walsh's head.

"I heard it all. Come on," Eli said. No, Walsh thought. *No, not like this*. His gut felt bottomless. Eli's brow never wavered. He showed no weakness and led Walsh by the ear, throwing the bag over his shoulder and escorting the killer back to Rock Springs.

Before the trial, the remains were brought down and laid to rest in the town cemetery. Upon further examination of the stolen gold, they found that it wasn't gold at all. It was fool's gold, a shiny counterfeit. Bobby never could tell the difference. Knowing that fact never made Walsh apologize.

I remembered the stories I had been told about Walsh. When he stood at the foot of the gallows, my knuckles tightened. He seemed more like a wolf than a man. His haunches shifted from side to side as he marched to the spot. He looked out onto the empty center of Rock Springs. He remained silent. I curtly asked him for his last words. He had none.

As soon as I pulled the mask over his face and tightened the noose, I pulled the lever. His large form crashed down, his feet hardly above the ground. I watched the top of his head, expecting a wriggle underneath the sack. He was gone, and I smiled. He was hanged by my hand and another dirty mongrel of Rock Springs was brought to rest.

## The Hanging of a Liar

Annabelle could feel the power of the early summer sun on her neck. She breathed deeply, taking in the sweet air after a long winter. She admired the glow of her yellow dress in the bright sunlight before dipping her pail into the well.

A scrawny young man walked around the farmhouse. On seeing her, he muttered rehearsed words, thrusting his feet forward slowly, one after the other. As he marched closer, his throat grew dry, suddenly unprepared. He mustered enough strength in his voice to get her attention.

"Good afternoon, Shane," Annabelle said.

"It's a beautiful day," he said, looking up at the

sky. She looked back to the well.

"It is..." She managed. Shane inched closer to her, looking at her with love in his eyes. He hoped she could feel the warmth he had for her in his heart, even when she looked away.

"Not as beautiful as you."

She dropped her hand from the pail. She faced him, examining his face. He was hopeful, yet sad.

"William's asked me to marry him."

"That's why I'm here. I love you, Annabelle. I love you more than anyone or anything in this world."

"Please, Shane." She stepped back.

"Didn't you hear me? I love you. I've always loved you. I promise you all the love a man can give. Everything I can give you, you'll have."

She probed his desperate, sorrowful eyes. *Can't you see?* she thought.

"I've promised William. I'm going to be his wife, not yours." Her fingers reached for her lips. *How could she have said that?* Shane's eyes lowered; his shoulders fell. His hand began to tremble, and his fingers twisted into a fist.

"But I love you, Annabelle. He can't love you as much as me."

"Please..." Frozen in fear, she waited, silently

begging him to walk away. *Please*. His hand shook as he tipped his hat.

"Don't tell William," he muttered. His pride couldn't be saved. He turned about face, almost stumbling. He was lost for words. He thought he'd never speak again. His sad march sent a chill down Annabelle's spine. Suddenly, the sun retreated behind a patch of clouds.

Dayton's main street was busier than usual. Summer was on the way. Oxen and carriages churned up the mud in the street. Annabelle waited in front of the general store. She looked over the heads and faces of the crowd. The clock wouldn't strike twelve for another three minutes. How could she wait any longer? Suddenly, a flash of dark hair crossed the street. She'd recognize him anywhere. His smile lifted his mustache, and his eyes fixed on her yellow dress.

"Darling," William whispered, taking her waist.

"My dear," she sighed. They shared a kiss, deaf to their rumbling little town. "Can't I see you tonight?"

"I'm sorry, darling. The fellas are holding the stag party tonight. It's only a week away."

"I know, but I can't wait..." She stroked his hand. "I've rented a room at the Silver Spur, upstairs. The owner doesn't know who I am. Nobody will know. I'll be there all night..." Their eyes met, burning with lust. Her fingers slipped past his hand, and she disappeared into the current of merchants and travelers.

The chill of night was unfelt as William and his friends shuffled from each saloon in town. Shane was red in the face, holding onto William's sleeve as he led them to the next house of debauchery. The Silver Spur waited for them on the other side of the street.

"Here's the next stop," William said, grinning ear to ear. The two other men were holding onto each other, finding their feet in the darkness.

"I... I think we got to find our way home, Willy!" The less drunk of the two said. The other man's head swayed.

"It looks like you fellas have reached your limit," William said. "Head home, you two."

"It's been a hollering good time." The drunken pair watched their steps and peeled off down the road. William kept his eye on the painted sign of a silver boot that hung over the next saloon.

"How about a nightcap, Shane?" Shane gave an affirmative grunt and followed him to the Silver Spur.

Inside was one barman, the owner, with a grisly beard and a potbelly, leaning against the bar, and another older man, hunched over his drink. William and Shane slid their stools under them and slapped the counter with their hard-earned money.

"You boys must've been drinking a lot tonight," the owner said.

"Not too much…"

"Not enough!" Shane declared. William gave his friend an uneasy look. He appealed to the barman for the mercy of another drink. The potbellied man sniffed and took the money off the table.

"Twelve cents, fellas," he said.

"Twelve cents?" William shouted.

"That's right," the owner said, nonchalantly waiting for an answer. Shane found a quarter before William thought to look and handed it to the man. A pair of beers and a penny slid across the counter to them.

"To a great night I think I'll forget," Shane slurred.

"I'm glad to have you as my best man," William confided in his inebriated friend. With a pat on the back and a knock of their glasses, they threw back a few beers. William kept his eye on his watch, as it grew closer to midnight. His eyes scanned the bar. *Think*! Fortunately, Shane slipped off his stool and walked out the back. William watched him go.

"Another round for my friend," he said to the owner. The large man turned around and poured another glass. William placed a coin on the bar and walked up the stairs. The barman turned around and thought nothing of it.

While Shane was relieving himself in the back alley, the old man at the bar ran his hand on his cold glass of beer. He dug into his pocket and plucked a quarter out of it. He slapped it on the hard oak.

"One more," he grumbled. The owner took the money and turned his back. A long silver revolver appeared from the old man's black jacket. The hammer cracked back. The barman knew what it was and what was about to happen.

"Take the money out and put it on the bar."

The owner threw as many dollars as he could into one hand. His club was next to the register, within arm's reach.

"I ain't got all night!" The old man growled. In an instant, the barman turned and slammed the thief with his club. The deafening roar of a revolver filled the saloon. The owner crashed to the floor and, before he knew it, his heart had stopped. Blood spilled out onto the money. The thief nearly fell behind the bar as he reached over and took all the money he could. Shane opened the back door and saw a dark figure run out the front. William and Annabelle came down the stairs quietly. They looked out the door and then saw Shane. Shane felt his jaw drop. Galloping hooves followed soon after.

Lanterns were lit. The sheriff and his deputies led the gauntlet to the Silver Spur. Townsfolk peeked out their windows and watched from the street. Finding Shane and the young couple inside, the sheriff and his men wrenched Shane out of the saloon. Annabelle screamed in protest. William and Annabelle chased after them.

"I didn't kill anyone! I'm not a murderer!" Shane shouted.

"He didn't do it!" Annabelle cried. William watched the sheriff's posse toss Shane forward.

"Don't worry, Shane! We'll tell them everything!" William projected. He wasn't sure if Shane could hear him over the sheriff's commands and the crowd's murmuring.

The sheriff and his deputies surrounded Shane as they forced him into a chair. Candles flickered around the room. The sheriff waved off his deputies. They shuffled out, leaving Shane and the sheriff to themselves. Shane could hear the uproar from the townsfolk outside. The sheriff's deputies shouted orders and stood firm before the door closed. The sheriff had his eyes on Shane this whole time.

"What's your name?" He asked.

"Shane Butler, sir."

"Do you live around here?"

"Yes, sir, on a farm nearby."

"Then how come I've never seen you before?" The sheriff asked, twirling a toothpick between his teeth.

"I like to stay out of trouble," Shane said with a chuckle.

"You're in trouble now, aren't you, boy?"

Shane's eyes widened. He held his breath and waited for the sheriff to break his gaze. Shane noticed the cold wind creep into the room. They waited for each other to speak, to make some admission.

"Where did you throw the gun?"

"I... I never carried a gun into town, sir. Honest," Shane begged. "If you question the other two, I mean my..."

"Who are you talking about?"

"My friends, they left before I got to the Silver Spur."

"They can testify that you weren't armed?"

"Yes, sir, I didn't do it. Please, you have to believe me." His eyes grew wet and vulnerable.

"If you didn't do it, who did?"

Shane looked down. It must have been the other man in the bar. Then he had another thought, one that constricted his throat. He faced the sheriff again and spoke clearly.

"It was William. He had an argument with the owner. He thought I'd left and that's when I saw him do it." The sheriff sat back in his seat, turning over the facts in his mind. Shane's face drooped in exhaustion.

"He's a friend of yours, is he?"

"Yes, sir."

"It's not easy to testify against your friends," the sheriff admitted. He looked into Shane's eyes, unsure of what he might find. "I won't need anything else from you. You've done your part." The sheriff pushed himself out of his chair and led Shane to the door.

The crowd had disappeared. William and Annabelle watched Shane as he appeared in the torchlight. William desperately examined his friend's face to glean any detail about what had happened inside. The sheriff planted his sight on William.

"You're under arrest," the sheriff declared. His deputies stepped forward with manacles. "You are under suspicion for robbery and murder."

William's face was agonized. In his mind, he was splashing in the deepest depths, only his face floating above the surface. Then it washed over him. It was clear to understand. His reticent eyes lowered to the manacles. They labored upward only to be punished by the stern determination of the sheriff who knew he had his man. He found himself shuffling his feet forward into the sheriff's office as they dragged him to his cell.

Shane hoped Annabelle would remain ignorant. His eyes held a sad hopefulness, hers a fiery hatred. He felt a blow to his core. Seeing the woman he loved hate him so passionately made him feel naked and ashamed but not enough to recant his witness. A yellow flash flew past him. The deputies restrained her. Shane ignored her cries of denial. The deputies shoved her outside and guarded the door. Shane let the moonlight guide him home, trying to keep his mind silent along the way.

"Let me by!" She cried. The deputies blocked the

door. They crossed their arms, and the middle one grew a nefarious grin.

"Not yet... But I think we can make some kind of arrangement..." He looked to his fellow deputies with that wolfish smile. Annabelle waited, knowing there was more, more that she couldn't refuse.

"We'll let you speak with him, as long as you save us a dance." They laughed. Annabelle stood her ground, hoping the embarrassment would be over soon. She hated them and their six eyes, leering at her. She was so dispirited that all she could do was nod, holding back a tear. They made a narrow gap for her to slip through.

When Annabelle brushed past the deputies, they let her whisper to her love, under their vigilant watch.

"Annabelle..."

"I'm here, darling." She pressed her hand against his cheek. "They can't do this to you. It isn't fair!" Annabelle pled. William wrapped his fingers around hers.

"I can't tell them what happened."

"Yes, you can. We'll run off together!"

"No, I won't do that. We have nothing, Annabelle. Where would we go?"

"I don't want to stay here without you. They'll hang you; you know that?" William stroked her finger and thought deeply.

"I can't ruin your name. No preacher'll marry us if they knew."

"We can run away. We don't need anybody."

"Where can I run to?" He asked. Her eyes took in the bars. She felt the barrier underneath her hands. Her eyes welled up, and her face twisted. William touched her face. She tried to compose herself. It was impossible, she knew. She couldn't bring herself to believe in hope. They never had a chance.

Two days later, I arrived and assembled the gallows. Once the deputies knew that I was finished they scattered across town and turned out every drunkard and gossiper they could find. Soon most of the town came to the feet of the gallows.

The door of the sheriff's office opened, revealing a young man who was resilient and strong, at least for a moment. When the deputies forced his first step, his eyes began to water. His head fell down and his feet hardly left the ground. The crowd parted for him and the deputies. Their eyes traced him; they were curious. The deputies made the march long, long enough for the crowd to see the crestfallen criminal.

He balked at the foot of the gallows. The

deputies forced his shoulders forward. He threw his head back and met my eyes. He was suddenly pale, struck by the sight of me. He seemed so much younger than me in that moment. Tears flanked his mustache, and the deputies pressed him into my arms.

I led him to the spot and laced the noose around his neck. The sheriff stared up at William. He was helpless; his eyes begged, reaching out for mercy. The sheriff felt eager for justice, and he showed William no shame in that fact.

"Do you have any last words?" I whispered. William began to shake. He searched through the crowd. He looked past faces new and familiar and wondered where she was; but she was there. As sure as the rising sun, she was there, on the corner of the platform at the general store. Her bottom lip held her fingertips. What could she say now? He sobbed bitter tears, dreaming of a future that would not be.

"If there is anything you would like to say…" I was patient. I waited for William to say his piece.

"I did…" His words broke into sobs. The townsfolk waited for his words. All anger was lost. They waited. William's back straightened and he stomped his foot. I stepped to him, masked his crying eyes with the burlap sack, and tightened the rope.

Before I lowered the lever, I felt relief. I had

given him his chance to speak. There was a solemn peace over the town. He died with dignity.

Annabelle turned away as he fell through the chute. She disappeared behind the general store and wept as she walked around town, alone.

She returned to her family home near sunset. Mud streaked across her shoes, her legs ached, and sweat slipped off her arms. She threw her head into her bedclothes and inhaled, rasping through heartsick lungs.

Shane never left the house that day. He couldn't sleep. He wondered what the execution was like, if William had cried in defiance of his fate, or if the deputies would arrest him after learning of his cruel trick. He hoped his friend expired without a word, and that made his stomach plunge within him.

When the darkness came over his farm, Shane let the window up in his bedroom. The cold night air crawled onto his feet. His head rested against the pillow. The thin bedclothes covered his torso as his legs twitched and peddled into place. He breathed. He sighed. He tried to deafen his own thoughts, keep his mind empty and dark. At some forgotten moment in the night, he fell asleep.

Shane woke to an open gray sky over his bed. He felt the bedclothes curl in his fingers. Two walls manifested at his sides, then another at his feet. He felt trapped. He tried to climb out, but the walls were made of dark soil and crumbled in his hands. He swung his vision to the clouds and found a congregation in black.

They sang in Latin or murmured beyond his comprehension. A withered, tight-skinned preacher stepped closer to the edge. He lifted his hands, and a rope lowered down. There was nothing but rope at first, and then he saw a pair of feet. The gray and bruised feet of decaying flesh descended into Shane's grave as the rope spooled at his side.

The body turned around the rope again and again until it stopped at the bottom of the grave facing Shane. Shane could see its eyes. There was no denying it. It was the corpse of William. His lifeless, marble eyes were all Shane could see. The rest of the world, the gray skies, and the faithful congregation disappeared, and Shane was alone with the black soil and William's rotting remains. William lay there with his crooked neck. His eyes never wandered.

Shane thrust himself forward, awake, lost,

disoriented, like he was drowning in a lake on a moonless night. His clothes stuck to him from the sweat, and he was chilled to the bone as the soft, slow wind dragged its frigid embrace into the room.

He muttered all of this to his family, then to the deputies. When I was preparing for my day at my home, I heard a knock at the door. I answered, and the postman had the same content expression on his face. He never read the messages he delivered. I looked at the letter, and it read: *A false witness claimed William Porter committed robbery and murder. Shane Butler will be hanged the day after you arrive.*

After reading that note I looked out onto the open plains from my doorstep where only the grass and sky lay. They were hanging the man who lied, but not the murderer. That man, whoever he was, was living a life of pleasure and freedom while these two fools hanged in his stead. The execution date was open to my arrival, but they trusted me. They knew I would do the job without question.

## The Hanging of Three Indians

The Indian Wars always seemed far away or all but over when I was a boy. I thought that the land was settled and that was that, whether the Indians liked it or not. Some of the Cheyenne were still fighting from caverns in the high mountains of western Wyoming. The soldiers chased them down by climbing after them, usually only one coming back.

Lieutenant Briggs dug his leather-gloved hand into the fresh snow. He crawled over the top of the cliff and came face to face with fresh tracks. Several smooth footsteps were imprinted in the snow. He made room away from the edge for his men. Twenty soldiers in total climbed up to the narrow cliff and followed their lieutenant. A cavern's black mouth watched the men as they formed into position. Briggs hid behind a rock nearby and reloaded his revolver.

The cavern made a sound. How many are in there? Briggs thought. One of his bullets fell into the snow. Briggs cursed and whipped his head to the cavern. He could hear them, or was that the sound of his heart pounding in his ears? *How many more could be left?*

"Come out of there!" Briggs roared. The wind stopped. Their breath hung in the air. Briggs clamped the hammer down on his revolver. "Hands in the air, and we won't fire!"

There was no answer. The men adjusted their rifles and hesitated to blink. What would surface from the darkness? Peering into the black, a face revealed itself. An Indian with a bow in hand stepped into the light. A revolver inside a holster was tied to the downcast bow. Two more followed on his flanks. Their weapons dropped into the snow.

Briggs waved his men forward. He stepped from behind his rock and kept his eyes trained on the first brave. He tried to watch all of them at once, never looking away from the first one who surrendered, the leader.

"Manacles!" Briggs shouted. A private ran

behind the Indians and bound their hands in iron traps. The other soldiers could feel the heat leaving their bodies. The fighting was over. They brought their prisoners back to camp, away from the frigid mountains.

The hanging was scheduled in the town of Morrison. Fort Washakie was nearby, but the officers agreed that it would be entertaining and heartening for the people to see that their soldiers were protecting them. Six men escorted the prisoners to the town jail, turning heads and eliciting gasps from the townsfolk. The soldiers were given leave during their stay. Half watched over the Indians the first night, and then took in the local debauchery the second night.

Building the gallows was hard enough, but the major insisted on executing the three prisoners at once. The wet slop they called Main Street was not the strongest foundation. After the mud dried to my skin and the scaffold, I heard shrill whispers behind me. The soldiers gave the word to bring out the prisoners. The idle men and women of Morrison turned into a crowd and began to gather, streaming in from the alleys and shops, creating a gauntlet for the walking dead.

The boos and sneers were almost immediate. Three stout, strapping men of varying ages were brought forward. They didn't seem like the portraits I had seen in newspapers. They wore more than loincloths, but they did have the same copper skin and eagle eyes that we were promised.

The small parade of prisoners trudged through the mud, dodging spit and bottles. The shame and sense of defeat were easily seen on their faces. Their stained moccasins stomped up the stairs to the gallows. The ropes were just long enough for their necks. The crowd started to move closer, packing the street.

"Any last words?" The major asked. The last one spoke to the others in their language. They answered him with grunts that must have meant something. "Well?" The major probed.

The first one looked ahead and spoke in his language. The crowd had perplexed looks on their faces. He saw that they could not understand, but he kept speaking. Then the next did the same. The spectators seemed to decide that it was a kind act to patiently give them their last say before the execution. When the second Indian said his piece, the third cleared his throat and spoke in English.

"I speak your language, and I will tell you what

they said." The townsfolk watched and listened. "My youngest brother said that he wishes doom upon you." The crowd's voice exploded in fury and mutual passion. "My cousin said that he hopes that your victory over our people is bittersweet and that the grass grows over your graves and the snow buries your houses." The same guttural bellow came from the crowd as it did before.

"Get on with it!" One of the soldiers said.

"I have other words for you to hear. I can understand how you think. I know your history. I know that you have made homes here that you cherish, as we cherish the memories of living in these green fields. Was there not enough room for our tribes...truly? Did we need to be swept away for your comfort? Did you have to kill us before chasing us into the mountains? And when we were there, why did you have to hunt us down? You had the land. When you had your war with the English, did you not fight back? Of course, you did. When the English burnt your cities to the ground, did you surrender? When they killed your sons and your fathers, did you want peace? Freedom is what you fought for; aestome means 'free' in our language, and that is what we want to be. You did not give up, so why do you think we must? We fought for our tribe, but we had no quarrel with yours, not until these past few years. Remember that the fruit from these trees is watered in blood."

The major gave me the order. I pulled the lever. Two fell without worry, but the one who spoke English was struggling. His legs kicked and his knees waved back and forth, trying to find another chance at life. He twisted and bucked. Only until I saw his body grow still did I hear the cheers from the townspeople.

The mortician and I cut them down. The mud-splattered corpses weighed more than we had thought they would. Their cheap caskets were laid down in shallow graves not more than fifty yards from town. The mortician said a prayer, and I bowed my head, picking the mud chips from my hands. Our shovels spilled the mud and soil over the caskets. Tired and brooding, we left the dead to be remembered only by those who buried them.

## *The Hanging of a Vengeful Man*

A drought had blown down the town of Settler's Creek. For years, it was a bountiful sea of green grass. After no rain for two months, the summer squeezed their throats. The only water they could find was in the dusty well at the town's gate. The gray stones that were piled up to create the arch were starting to tumble one at a time. The wooden banner that hung over the arch was almost illegible and about to fall to one side.

A dark-haired woman tied her hair before stepping out into the street. She held a pail in each hand. She wiped the dust from the well's edge and sat lightly. She pulled on the rope and lifted the bucket to her side. She filled her first pail before lowering the rope again. A horse's hooves announced his master's presence. She looked up and shaded her eyes with her hand.

A middle-aged man dressed in a white tunic entered Settler's Creek with a pleasant smile surrounded by scruffs of hair. He had traveled a long while; his hair plateaued over his ears. She thought he was handsome but pitied his luck. She looked down into the well before he approached her.

"Do you think you could help me carry this up?" she said.

He tied his horse's reins to the stake next to the well. He rolled up his sleeves then reached into the well for the rope. His arms flexed and his hands juggled the rope up to her. She caught it and filled her pail. He let the rope slip through his hands as he stared into her eyes.

"Do you need anymore?" He asked.

She flicked her finger across the edge of her lip and stood up.

"No, this is enough, for the morning," she admitted.

"Maybe you can help me," he said. "I was looking for work, or at least a place to stay."

"I'm sorry to tell you that nobody is hiring any extra help. As you can tell, the rain has passed us over this summer."

"Well that's not what I meant to say. I mean… I mean that there might be work here. Is there an orphanage around here?"

"Yes, there is. We have about a dozen of them— the children I mean. I'm sure you heard about the wildfire a few years ago."

"Yes, that's a real shame. I would like to help there."

"Help? What do you mean?"

"If they need an extra pair of hands, I wouldn't need to do it for pay. I would just like to help." He wiped away the sweat growing on his brow.

She looked at him deeply. "I look after the orphanage, actually. You can follow me."

"Isn't that convenient? Like I said, there's no need for…"

"Follow me," she said.

He took his horse and marched behind her.

The orphanage was less than a mile from the town. The long yellow grass was wild and brushed against their legs. There were children in white play clothes with patches over the knees chasing each other in the field in front of the house. It was a two-story house with a ramshackle stable at its side.

The boys and girls ran around in a circle until they noticed Ruth and a strange man coming down the beaten lane. They whispered to each other, some hoped for a new father, others thought the man was the caretaker's brother. Before they could ask her about this man, Ruth directed him to tie his horse beneath the shade of the stable.

He entered the house, and the children streamed past him. The home was ornate and had brown carpets stretching across the floor and on the stairs. The curtains were pale with red headings. They had found a place on their walls for every painting and photograph. He admired the little decorations around the room; Ruth noticed her hair had lost its shape, and she tied it back into her preferred style.

"The ladder is out by the stable." She reached around a corner. "You'll have to climb up. The ladder isn't very tall." She handed him a bucket of nails and shingles with a hammer sticking out.

He took it without complaint or question. She smiled at that.

"Wait," she said. He stood in the threshold. "What do we call you?"

"You can call me Seth," he said. "What should I call you?"

"Ruth."

He smiled, nodded, and shut the door behind him. A sense of relief washed over her shoulders. It was nice to have someone who could do the work that needed to be done.

The house was struck by lightning during the last storm of spring, leaving a pair of holes in the roof. Seth took hold of the gutter with one hand and the tough, old sloped roof with the other. His arms and back strained as he pulled himself to the top. He turned himself around to reach for the bucket. His index and middle finger pinched the edge of it and brought it with him onto the roof with a wobble.

When the last nail plunged into the roof, Seth smoothed out the last shingle, turned around and sat. The wind blew over the yellow grass and whispered behind Seth's ears. He felt at peace on that rickety roof. His palms pressed down, and he took in the sun.

When the heat reached his face, he began to climb down. He found Ruth in the kitchen with the children. She had just prepared them a meal. Her eyes were patient.

She noticed Seth walk through. "There's a pump outside that needs fixing. Have you fixed a pump before?"

"Miss, I can do everything you ask of me, but I'll need three meals a day."

She was caught off guard. "Three? Do you plan to stay here at the house?"

"I could always stay at an inn."

"There isn't one," she said, casting her gaze at the floor.

Seth cleared his throat and shifted in his boots. "It's plenty warm outside…"

"Of course…" Their eyes met, waiting for the other to speak. "I'll fix you some food."

"You can do it after I fix that pump," he said. He walked past her and out the back door.

She watched him go.

The rusted pump had fallen apart like everything at that house. Seth worked at it as much as he could. The late afternoon sun was beating his neck raw. He was not exactly a handy man, but he looked over the pieces of the pump and figured his way around it. He tightened the screws with his hands. He experimented with his repairs to see if they had succeeded. The only hope he found from his work was that a small stream of water came out after his fifteenth crank of the machine.

Inside, Ruth watched. She'd meant to make him

a meal, to give him some time to rest, but instead she'd watched him work. With this new arrival, she put off the children's lessons for the day. They ran around in the front yard again. When his shoulders towered over the pump, she turned back and made herself busy. He opened the back door and waited for her to turn. She did with a doe-eyed expression.

"Have you finished?" she asked.

"I wasn't able to get much water out of it. I can run to the well in town for you, if you'd like."

"In the morning we will need some. Let me make you something," she said.

He found a seat at the table. The sweat was rolling over his body, but his face didn't show an ounce of strain.

After dinner, he went into town to wash by the well. He was nearly dry by the time he came back. He fed and brushed his horse until sunset. Ruth had no chores for him that evening, so he stayed outside with his horse until it was too dark. Ruth had sent the children to their room for the evening and lit a candle in the parlor to read a book until Seth returned to the house.

The door opened slowly, as if by the breeze, and

Seth saw Ruth by the light. She stood and snapped her book shut. The candle showed her full face as the grayish blue of dusk took over the house.

"There is a room upstairs," she said. "I saw you had a bedroll on your horse. You don't need to sleep outside, if you don't want to."

"I would appreciate that, Miss." She led him upstairs. There were three rooms on the second floor. Ruth's was the master bedroom, and Seth's would be in between her room and the children's.

"It's not much, but it will be nicer than sleeping outdoors." Seth stepped to the door. He looked inside and could make out a small bed and a small armoire to go with it. He looked out of the room and saw that Ruth was in the threshold of her own bedroom door.

She waited for him to go inside.

He shut the door and stepped towards her. She shrank back into her room, keeping him in her sights.

"Miss, it is very kind of you to let me stay here. I promise to get that pump fixed tomorrow."

Still hidden, she let the corner of her mouth rise.

"I'm sure you will... How long do you plan on staying?"

"Miss, I can..."

"You may call me Ruth."

"Very well, Ruth, I would like to stay for some

time. As long as I am useful, I would like to help you here."

"Why? Why this little place? Where did you come from?"

"I'm from Cheyenne. I came here because I came to a point in my life where I wanted to do something noble. As you can tell, I never married. I always felt something steering me away from that life, not that marriage wouldn't be good for me...but I'm getting older and I wanted to help where I can. I heard of this place, and I thought that I could make it worth your while."

"How did you hear about us?"

"After that fire, your town was in the newspaper. I was hoping to help here, and if this town needed anything, I would be another man to rebuild and get you all back on your feet..."

"Well I'm happy that you came our way," she stated.

He wanted to say more but saw in her eyes that he should go. He opened the door to his bedroom, and she blew out the candle.

Seth's hands ached from carrying water from the well. His shoulders felt locked in place. The children knocked over a bucket as Ruth dismissed them from breakfast. She tipped it back up and wanted to holler out to them, but they'd already run out of the house. Seth's hand felt like a claw that couldn't close or open, stuck in place. She took pity on him, knowing that he'd have to go back again.

There was work to be done that day. Ruth had a list of orders for him. The pump was an issue he couldn't begin to know how to fix. He tried anyway.

By noon, his faith in himself had dried up. He decided to move on to another chore. He took a scythe from the broken down stable and unhitched his horse. The elegant creature started to graze from the grass in front of the house. Seth began to swing the scythe around, folding the grass in front of him. By the end of the day, he had fifty yards of grass cut in a sea of gold.

Ruth lifted her head as he entered. His arms were oiled with sweat.

She became upset by the sight of his satisfied smile. She shooed the children out of the kitchen.

"What are you smiling about?" she asked.

"Do the children have lessons in the morning?" He asked, wiping his arms with a wet rag.

"Yes," she reluctantly said.

"I think a little education about sporting would

be a good idea for them. What do you say?"

"You've made yourself quite at home. The children will learn what *I* teach them. Do you not think I'm the one doing you a favor?"

"I thought a game of baseball would be a fun time for them. Don't you think they should have fun?"

"Just because you've given me a hand around here doesn't mean you can decide what is best for the children. Carrying water and fixing the roof aren't enough for you to decide what goes." Her steely eyes forced his eyes downwards.

His shoulders slumped. His smile lifted but only for a moment.

"I guess you're right," he said. "I don't mean to cause trouble. I'll get back to work on whatever you need tomorrow morning." He let the towel fall from his hands into the bucket. His footsteps echoed throughout the house and tapped against the wood of the stairs. Ruth moved the pails of water from the kitchen and made herself a small meal in silence.

Ruth woke to a soft pounding outside her window. She rose and pulled the curtains back to see Seth digging a large hole in the ground next to the pump.

He was about four feet past the surface and not slowing down.

After teaching her lesson to the children, they ran out to the front to play in the newly cut grass. She could still hear the shovel cutting into the earth. She kept an eye on the children as they ran around in the large square before walking into the kitchen to fetch a pail of water. She could still see Seth's arms throwing soil up to the surface.

Seth's horse was stripping the ground of grass from where he was tied. He was a pitiable thing. Seth's hard work had led to neglect of his beast. Ruth raised the pail to the horse's snout. The animal splashed the water around and drank as much as it wanted. She placed the bucket next to the post and started to untie him. Her eyes stayed with the creature at all times. She had never seen a horse that close before, close enough to feel its breath warm her arms.

The creature bowed its head and took bites from the long grass. Ruth stroked its neck. One of the girls fell to the ground, and the playing stopped. The children looked to Ruth for help. Ruth whispered to the horse. The playing continued.

Seth's arms were painted with soil. The stripes of

dark earth started to spill from his arms as he sweated in the sun. Ruth's tiny footfalls came from behind. He decided that eight feet down might be a good place to rest. He wiped his dirty forehead and looked at the lady of the house.

"I don't know how to fix a pump, but I know that if you dig deep enough you can start a well. You won't have to walk to town anymore."

"I see that. I fed and watered your horse for you."

"Why thank you, Ruth. If you're still fine with me calling you that."

She was amused but didn't show it. She kept her eyes on him in the well to be.

"You may," she allowed herself to say. "If you can do that, then I would be very thankful."

He smiled from down below. The wind didn't touch his hair, but hers began to flutter.

"I should be able to break water this afternoon."

"Good, would you like something to eat?"

"Sure, I would. Bring the ladder over."

She looked back to the wall and dragged it to the hole. She started to lean the ladder down, but Seth put his hands out in protest.

"No, that's alright. Just leave it next to the hole." She did as she was told and watched his hands grip the dry grass. His arms bulged and his chin caught the edge of the hole. His legs pushed him up and out with a fluid movement. He stood up with a satisfied smile right in front of her. She giggled and led him into the house.

When he struck the waterbed underneath the earth, it burst out like a wound. His feet were swamped, but he kept digging. The wet mounds were burdensome to throw. He could feel the bone in his shoulder drop from the weight. He threw the mounds to the top all the same. Until he could fill a bucket by standing it upright, he kept digging through the water into the pulpy under soil.

With mud-slicked wrists, Seth emerged from his well, exultant. He hoped that Ruth was watching, but he only saw the backside of the house. He sighed happily despite it and hoisted the ladder from the deep well. He washed himself from the last of the town's well water they would need. The wound in the earth sprang forth enough water to last them years of drought.

The crack of a stick sprawled out across the prairie

and was chased by the laughter of children. A little boy ran from one sandbag to the other. The ball started to fly back to the pitcher's mound. Seth's tough hands caught it with a clap and gave a low throwback to Ruth at home plate. The little boy had hit the base before she could catch it. Everyone cheered for his triumph.

A girl took her place at the plate, and Ruth stood behind her, holding the stick with her. Seth threw the ball softly towards them. Ruth held the girl tight and guided the bat to knock the ball between first and second. Ruth gave her a little push on the back to run. Every child on defense ran to the ball.

"Wait!" Seth shouted. "One of you has to stay on first base! She's going to be safe if she gets there!" The little blonde girl with her head tucked to her chest was already there before they could say Timbuktu. Her compatriots behind Ruth gave yelps and cries in her honor.

Tommy was the next boy to swing. He whirled the stick around and struck the ball with all his boyish strength. The ball flew over Seth's head and to the edge of the cut grass. Little legs went pumping and hearts started racing. Ruth stood back as they came around the last base.

Seth waved his arms to the boys to get the ball

back to him. They tried, but Tommy was running too fast. Seth's hands clamped down on the ball as soon as it arrived. He turned and tossed it to Ruth. She saw Tommy running at her; her frantic mind cut between him and the soaring ball. She grasped the ball and pulled it into her chest, but Tommy kept running. His charging elbow and shoulder knocked her over onto her rear.

Seth's heels sprang off the mound. He took Tommy's collar and held it like a vice.

"I'm sorry, Miss Ruth," he cried. Seeing the boy's tears made Seth loosen his grip. A shade of regret fell over his face when he surveyed the frightened faces of the children.

Ruth's nose started to run red. His mind was made up; the boy would be spared.

"Play quietly," Seth said. "The game is over." He picked Ruth up and onto her feet. He escorted her inside. Her arms trembled under his soft grasp as she saw the blood stain her fingers. Inside, she held as much of the blood in her hands, keeping her dress spotless. She sat in the kitchen and waited as Seth collected a bucket of water.

"It doesn't hurt too badly," Ruth said.

Seth rinsed a rag and brushed it against Ruth's nose. She thought of taking it herself but let him do it anyway. "I bet I look silly with a broken nose. It's not broken, is it?"

"No, I've seen worse. It would take more than that to do it."

"Thank you," she said. "Where did you see worse?"

He looked away from her.

She knew she shouldn't have asked.

He slipped the rag into her hands.

"I fought in the Civil War..." He washed his hands with a story on the edge of his tongue.

"Was it...difficult?" He wanted to tell her the truth, how it really was but thought against it.

"Parts of it were." That was enough, he decided.

She looked into the rag and weakly tapped it against her wounded nose.

"How do you make it work here?" He asked. "Before I came along, you didn't have anyone to help you."

"Well, there is someone who helps us. Pastor Meyer collects donations when he does his guest preaching around the territory. He'll be here tonight for dinner. Tomorrow's Sunday." Seth's eyes didn't change.

"Are you a believing man, Seth?"

He busied himself with examining her nose

before looking her in the eye.

"If he's been helping you out here, he's probably a man worth listening to." She grinned and applied the rag to her nose again. She looked back at him through her eyelashes.

"After I send the children up to bed, you can meet him. We usually have a nice talk afterwards." Seth nodded with a grunt and walked past her.

That night, when the moonlight gave the fields a cool glow, Ruth dismissed the children to their bedroom. Pastor Meyer was a young man with sandy hair and spectacles. He ate with his jaw sawing side to side. Other than that, he seemed like an unassuming, well-mannered, and bookish young man with a sacred profession.

"The little ones are off to bed now," Ruth said in a chipper voice. Seth looked at her while she said it. She said it only to the pastor.

"I'm happy to see they haven't lost their appetite. You're doing fine work, Ruth." He patted her on the hand.

"Thank you, Pastor."

"So, Seth, what were you doing before you came to town?"

Seth's irritated eyes didn't shift. They were on Pastor Meyer always.

"I fought in the war," he said.

"For the Union?" the pastor asked.

"I'm sure there's something else we could talk about," Ruth interrupted.

"That's right," Seth said, ignoring her.

"And what have you done since your service in the army?"

"I've worked here and there, whatever they would pay me for." Seth moved to finish the last portion of his meal.

"Oh, a man of the world, like what, for example?" The pastor locked his fingers.

Seth lost his appetite and licked his lips. "Railroads, mining, I moved from place to place, like I do now." He slopped the last of his food into his mouth.

"And your wife? What happened to her?"

Ruth touched the pastor's hand.

"Perhaps we shouldn't pry."

"I just want to know where our fellow sinner comes from." He looked at Seth with satisfied and reassured eyes. He knew. He must have known. Why torture him like this if he didn't enjoy it?

"I never married," Seth confessed.

"And what kind of work have you done for children? You must have done something to have such a gentle hand for the young."

"Please, pastor," Ruth implored.

"I like hearing stories like these," the pastor replied. "A path onto the straight and narrow, right, Seth?"

Seth said nothing, gleaning all he could from the pastor's expression.

"I'll take your dish, Seth," Ruth said. She took it while the two men looked at each other.

"We haven't met before, have we?" Seth asked.

"No, I don't think we have," the pastor said.

"What else did you see on your journey, pastor?" Ruth asked while rinsing the plates.

"It was a lonely journey, Ruth. There weren't a lot of people around, but they grew close. Closer than they might ought to be." Ruth looked back at her dishes in an instant, avoiding the pastor's eye.

"I should get back to town. I am very sore from the ride," the pastor said.

"Oh," Ruth said, wiping her hands on her dress. "It was nice to see you again. We will see you this Sunday."

"Of course," the pastor said as he stood. He showed himself to the door while Seth and Ruth followed. Seth kept his distance and watched him from across the room. Ruth made sure he had taken everything with him.

"Is there anything you would like to say to me before I go, Seth?"

"No." The pastor nodded and glided out the door with a self-righteous smirk.

The next morning was as dry as any since Seth had come to town. He and Ruth had several pails with them as they rode on his horse. It would be the last of the town's well water that they would need. The well at the back of the house was doing its job. Ruth needed some food from town, so they made a trip of it.

Seth's brawny arms yanked at the rope of the well. The high heat kept the drops of water from staying too long on his body. His horse picked at the grass around the well. He didn't hear the horseman coming to the gate of Settler's Creek. When Seth looked up, he recognized the horseman immediately.

The man dropped from his horse and turned his hands to fists.

"You come looking for me?" Seth asked.

"Sure as hell I've come looking for you," the

man said. His right hand lowered toward a black revolver.

Seth spat and stood tall. "I left looking for something better to do. I can't take all your money playing cards."

"You think I came all this way because you beat me in a game of cards?"

"What do you want, George?"

Ruth began brushing the horse's head. She watched Seth and the stranger, listening intently.

"I see you've made quick work of things," George said, looking Ruth's way.

"What are you talking about?"

"I know why you wouldn't want to tell her. It's why you went away. I know what you did, Seth! I heard you do it!"

"Who is this man, Seth?" Ruth asked.

He waved her off.

"Nobody, just stay behind the horse."

"You got her drunk, didn't you?" George spat. "You took her away and...and you soiled her. I heard it all. I didn't know it until she told me. That's why I came here." He drew his weapon and snapped the hammer back.

"You're wrong about him," Ruth hollered from behind the horse.

"That's enough, Ruth." Seth turned back to George, keeping his eye on the barrel pointed at him.

"You don't know him as well as I do, Miss."

"He's helped me take care of the children at the orphanage outside of town. You don't know who this man truly is."

"He raped the woman I love, and he did it just to spite me. He did it for his own sake. I knew him for a long time. You think you can trust a man after a short while, but you can't. You don't know the whole truth, the real truth about the man. Any last words, Seth?"

"Don't shoot!" Ruth pled.

"He doesn't deserve it. Whatever life he has now, he doesn't deserve it."

"You didn't deserve her," Seth rebuked. "She never wanted to marry you, and you know it."

"She loved me, and you took her in your foul way."

"You were a coward then and a coward now. I've made my troubles, but I've left that behind."

"You don't get to walk away from what you've done. You get yours, one day or another." He adjusted his grip on the revolver. "I hope you die slow, you son of a bitch."

The bullet ripped through Seth's chest. Ruth screamed in the horrid way mothers mourn their children. She crawled to him and clutched at his clothes, watching his eyes fade away from hers.

George Whitfield was hanged the next day. The judge was borrowed, and the jury was made up of witnesses. Ruth wore black and didn't say a word. After the noose burned around his neck, it began to rain. Small drops at first and then it came in sideways, uprooting the soil and washing it clean.

# *The Hanging of the McClellan Brothers*

Most think that western Nebraska has nothing to offer but farmland. The people of Cheyenne learned in a short afternoon that was not the case. The noon train to Cheyenne was running on schedule. There was one car of passengers and the rest were filled with cargo. Nebraska was almost behind them.

As soon as the locomotive flashed past a ranch, four horsemen chased after it. Two raced on either side, catching up to the passenger car. They wore black masks under their eyes. One pair of horses moved closer, the wheels threatening to chip at their hooves. Before jumping on, the elder brother turned to the younger.

"Ride as fast as you can to Cheyenne! With all the horses!"

The younger man was exhilarated. It was time to do his part.

"I will!" He shouted back, suddenly feeling a cold weight drop in his stomach.

His brother fell silent. The elder looked to the platform car directly behind the car full of travelers. He kicked his horse twice and lifted himself onto its back. He clutched the bar on the platform with one hand and swung himself over. He looked back to his brother. His faith was reassured as his brother took hold of his horse. He gave a curt wave. His younger brother faded out of sight behind the train as it curved along the tracks.

The other horsemen neared the car. The elder brother gave his hand. The first was a large man with a red beard that grew past his mask. The last one was blonde with piercing blue eyes.

"Thanks, Merrill," the bearded one said. "Zeke, Andy, are you ready?" he asked.

Zeke cracked his knuckles and nodded. Andy's blue eyes said enough. Merrill took a deep breath before he tried his hand on the door of the passenger car. It opened smoothly and the passengers looked back.

"Hands in the air!" Merrill unbuckled his revolver from his holster and thrust it forward. A woman screamed before her husband enclosed his arms around her.

"Do what he says!" Zeke roared.

The crowd's arms jolted upward.

"All the men stand up!"

Some of the men stood right away, others took their time. One near Merrill wouldn't budge.

"Hands up!" Merrill sounded off at the uncompromising passenger.

Zeke dug his revolver into the man's skin. The man stretched upward and frowned, despondent about his choices. Andy saw the conductor, frozen in place at the front of the car. The conductor raised both hands in the air, sinking more hearts into despair.

Merrill moved to the cowardly conductor and shoved him to the back. Zeke took the conductor by the back of the neck and trapped him in the corner of the car. The passengers watched their captor, and he watched them, dissuading any heroics with his stark gaze. Merrill looked at the men in the car. Some were terrified; others were stoic. He glanced at their waists; none were armed.

"Very good, gentlemen," Merrill said.

His eyes revealed the smile hiding under his mask. "Everyone, just hand over your money and then sit down and enjoy the ride." Andy held the bag and pointed his weapon at the first passenger. She placed some coins inside it. Her husband handed over a few dollars before sitting down. By the time Andy had robbed every passenger, the train's whistle screeched to the sky. Cheyenne was only a few miles away.

"All the men," Merrill announced. "Get to the back!"

Wives grasped at their husband's arms, but a second boom of Merrill's voice kept the men moving. With over a dozen men in the back of the car, Andy, Merrill, and Zeke stepped to the middle of the car and whispered to each other while Zeke kept his eye on the prisoners.

"Zeke, you need to stay back," Merrill said. "Watch the men and don't let any of them leave or make a sound."

Zeke steadied his glare on the prisoners.

"And the horses?" Andy asked.

"We'll have to wait a while. You said there was a bank that's close to the station?"

"It's almost right across the street from it."

"All right, we can ju—" The train slowed and

lurched forward before stopping. It sighed as steam escaped its undercarriage. Merrill walked to the front of the car and took a young lady by the arm. She gasped, and her husband stood up.

"Sit down," Zeke barked. The click of his revolver's hammer sent the man back to the floor. Andy took the arm of another woman.

"No, please!" She cried. She slapped his arm, but he pulled her off her feet and dragged her behind Merrill.

Merrill told his prisoner to open the door. She quickly clutched the handle and sprung it open. The unlikely couples walked to the engineer's cabin. Luckily, the engineer stepped out of his quarters as they approached.

"Don't move," Merrill ordered. "Do exactly as I say."

The engineer was dumbstruck. His mind shot back and forth between his options. Taking his chances, he jumped back to the door to his cabin.

Merrill boxed his ear and pressed the revolver against his head. "Do as I say," he said through gritted teeth.

"Yes, all right, all right," the engineer muttered. He touched his throbbing, bleeding ear.

"Take him too," Merrill said to Zeke as he

shoved the engineer into the passenger car. Then he gripped the woman's arm and gave it a twist. She cried in pain. Zeke stepped out of the aisle and motioned the bloody engineer to join the others. The engineer's left hand held the other, trying to stop his trembling. The passengers' eyes grew in fear after seeing the engineer in his condition.

Cheyenne was bigger than Merrill had guessed, even from Andy's description. The buildings were taller than most he had seen, and the streets had more carriages than he could count. Faces began to creep past corners, and Merrill's head whipped around.

"Where's the bank, Andy?"

"It's coming up. Don't panic." They pushed the women ahead and stood them up with the cold barrels on their backs. There were too many people on the street, too many witnesses. Merrill hoped every door would lead to the bank, but Andy kept pushing forward. Finally, they reached the double doors of the Bank of Cheyenne. The faces were still watching them.

"Open it!" Merrill gave a harsh whisper to the girl. She leaned into the door and rushed through it.

"This is a robbery!" Merrill shouted. "Patrons get

down on the floor! Clerks put your hands up! Keep them up!"

Two men crouched on the ground and one clerk reached for his keys. He opened the gate to allow them entrance. Merrill and Andy forced themselves in. The clerks began to slide dollars and coins into the bag. Merrill looked around at the customers on the floor.

"Don't move!" Merrill warned. The men shuddered and pressed their faces to the floor. Andy watched as the men shoved money into the bag. Its size grew and drew his wrist back with its weight.

"This is a fair take. We should be fine with this," Andy said with a semblance of a smile under his mask. Merrill wrenched the girl around the counter. Andy held open the bag for Merrill to see. Their newfound wealth cleansed his tired eyes.

"Take as much as you can carry," Merrill said with his mouth hanging open.

"This is all I can take," Andy said.

"What about the girl?" Merrill asked. Andy looked at his occupied hands and then to the captive woman.

"We're just a pair of gentlemen making a withdrawal," he said as he slipped his revolver into his holster with a click. Merrill smiled and dragged his hostage with him. Andy twisted the top of the sack of money and looked to his prisoner. Her dark eyes held their focus and shed tears without distraction. He took her by the small of her back and waltzed her through the door.

The men crowded in the back of the train car tried to rest without rising, but their knees ached from squatting and kneeling. Zeke would trail them with the barrel of his revolver whenever one of them rose above his waist. A young man scratched his forehead and took off his hat to wipe the sweat from his brow.

"Hey!" Zeke shouted. "Don't move! What did I tell you?"

The man shook in fear. He placed the hat on his head like a feather falling to the ground. The engineer looked at the conductor sitting next to him. Their eyes met and looked to the door behind them. Then they looked at Zeke's massive hand holding his weapon. The conductor looked at the engineer with a fear that ran through his core. The engineer nodded with narrowed eyes. His partner nearly swallowed his tongue. The engineer turned his head to their tormentor.

"Do you think you can run from this?" the

engineer asked.

Zeke adjusted his grasp on the revolver. "Do you want to keep us from running?"

"You can't leave the station without my help. I am your only way out. Your only escape," he said.

Zeke looked out the windows, hoping to see Merrill and Andy.

The engineer tapped the conductor on the leg and pointed with his thumb to the door.

"There's more than one way to leave Cheyenne," Zeke said. He liked the sound of that and licked his bottom lip. Another man lifted his hat. Zeke's gun followed him.

"There won't be another way out if you harm any of us. The sheriff or the marshals will find your tracks, wherever you go," the engineer said. The conductor's mustache lifted with delight. He had hope.

"No more talking from you," Zeke said.

"Are you sure about that?" The engineer dared.

Zeke stomped forward, and the conductor made his move. The train car's rear door swung open and Zeke discharged his weapon. The engineer's head flung around; his eyes focused on the upright heels of his partner. He thought he would shake when he saw a man killed in front of him, but he was too scared to think of it. Zeke pulled the hammer again. The resolute snap made the engineer's head spin.

"See what happens when you don't play by the rules?" Zeke asked.

The engineer prayed in silence, his breath suspended by the anticipation of a blast of light from the revolver.

It didn't come.

Exposed in the midday sunlight, the two thieves looked around to orientate themselves. Their heads pivoted around the streets of Cheyenne to see a familiar building or street corner. Everything seemed new. They couldn't focus with their nerves on edge, money in hand, and hostages in tow. A loud clap from behind forced their desperate eyes toward the train station.

A woman made a horrible cry as she witnessed a man fall out of the passenger car. Her feet carried her as far away from the scene as they could. Merrill begged for a carriage to appear before them. The streets were emptied as men and women hid and scattered.

"Dammit! Where do we go?" Merrill asked.

Andy looked into the train car and saw Zeke

threatening the passengers with his revolver. "Zeke!" Andy called.

The giant backed away from the crowd of crying women and terrified men. His revolver had an approximate mark on all of them as he opened the door to hear Andy more clearly.

"What is it?" Zeke shouted, looking back inside to make sure no others escaped.

"We have to go! We need to find some horses!"

"Where's James?"

"It doesn't matter!" Merrill boomed.

"Why don't we just take the train? We have the engineer right here!"

"They'll stop us in the next town!" Andy explained.

"Let's move!" Merrill ordered.

Zeke took one look back at his captives and grunted as he left the train. Merrill yanked his hostage over and ran with her along a long road. Andy and Zeke followed.

"Pick up the pace, woman!" Merrill shouted. She was tripping on her dress. Merrill took a handful of it and handed it to her. Andy and Zeke took their girl in each arm and nearly carried her off the ground as they ran. Every alley and street were a misfortune. The streets only held witnesses in paralyzed fear as they flashed past them.

Merrill slowed down at a junction closer to the center of town. Andy and Zeke stopped behind him. Their damp palms and searching eyes were driving them mad for safety. Andy looked behind them and around every corner.

"Merrill, the sheriff is bound to find us any minute. We need a plan," Andy begged.

"Where can we hide?" Merrill asked the prisoners. They were both gasping for air. Any amount of distraction would give them time for the authorities to find them.

"Answer him!" Zeke said with a clap on the back of their necks.

"There's an old barn near here. I promise!" She pointed the direction to follow. The streets were silent as they ran. Cheyenne was not a large city, but folks could lose direction easily. Aside from the panting and footfalls, it almost seemed empty, deserted, until they heard the horses chasing after them. The sheriff and his deputies knew who they were. There was no mask they could wear without being known.

Zeke blew two bullets down the street. The woman on Andy's arm flew off with a scream into an alley. Being exposed, Andy felt a punch in his gut.

He was in danger. He turned back to his enemies and fired away at the oncoming horses. His defense toppled a man from his horse. Zeke struck another man down, but the deputy aimed back at them as soon as he bounced off the ground.

The sheriff and his men careened out of the street to avoid the gunfire. The deputy that had fallen off his horse took cover behind a stoop and discharged his weapon. Zeke plummeted to the ground with a groan. Andy shot back in wild anger. The deputy slid underneath the step. Andy could have sworn he was dead, but he couldn't see.

"We have the girl!" Merrill shouted. The dust settled. Andy set down the money and retrieved Zeke's gun from his cool hand.

"Drop your weapons and let the lady go!" The sheriff shouted.

Andy held the two revolvers clumsily in one hand and took the sack of cash in the other. Merrill didn't reply and ran to the barn. The sheriff fired at them. The revolvers flew from Andy's hand. He collapsed and sprawled out past the corner of the barn. He crawled into cover and flipped onto his back. A bleeding hole in his leg seeped out. He gave a shout and began to shake.

"Don't worry, I've got you," Merrill said. He

placed his revolver on the ground and took his friend by the shoulders. The young woman ran off around the corner. She screamed to the sheriff. He waved her over to him. Merrill opened the barn door and took the fallen bag of money and revolvers inside, before dragging his fellow bandit to safety. Andy tried to hold back his pain, but it was written all over his face. A painted trail followed them with grunts and groans. Merrill closed and bolted the door. The only light that came in was from a glassless window on the north side of the barn.

Andy padded his leg with some loose hay. Merrill shuddered at the sight of his friend, half in darkness and soon to be half stained in blood. Merrill dragged their supplies to his friend and sat against the bale of hay with him.

"How many bullets do you have left?" Merrill asked, checking their chambers.

"I lost count, Merrill. You're going to have to count them."

"You need to remember. You only have six to fire. You don't want to run out."

"How many did you fire?" Andy asked in a concerned tone. Merrill was busy counting bullets in the weak light.

"You fired twice, and Zeke fired four times. That

leaves you with four in this one," Merrill placed the gun into his friend's weak grip. "And two in this one." He set Zeke's on the ground between them.

"What's the next part of the plan?" Andy asked.

"They'll have us surrounded. They might try to break the door down. It looks like we'll have to shoot our way out."

"We don't need to do that."

"I know you're hurt, but we've got to get out of this town."

"I don't. You can climb out of here. I can't run with you."

"We can fight our way out. Do you really want to go to prison for this?"

"What the hell am I supposed to do?" Andy boomed. Three knocks pounded on the door. Their heads snapped to the sound. Merrill had his revolver ready. Andy slowly raised his. The sheriff and his men tried to open the barn door.

"There's no way out! Unlock this door and come out unarmed!" The sheriff ordered.

Merrill looked to his bleeding friend. "I don't want to put you in harm's way, Andy."

"I'd understand if you wanted to take them down. I might too if I were you instead of me."

"Open up in there!" The sheriff bellowed.

"We need to decide, Andy. What do you say?" Andy handed Zeke's revolver to Merrill.

"I'm not running anywhere. You'll need all the help you can get." Merrill stood up and prepared his weapons with stiff cranks on the hammers. He moved behind a bale of hay and aimed towards the door.

"As soon as they open, you need to shoot with me, you understand?" Merrill said.

"I will." Andy sat up straight and pointed his weapon at their enemies. There was a shuffling of feet outside the door.

"Stay back!" The sheriff warned.

Merrill ducked and kept his eyes pried open.

"Don't come any closer! Get back! Nobody else needs to get hurt!" The voice turned towards the door. "Do you hear that, boys? This whole town's had enough of your trouble. They've come prepared in case you do anything nasty. Don't spill any more blood than you already have. Come out quietly and no harm will come to you."

Merrill's eyes glanced to Andy's figure, rooted to the spot. Merrill's hammers clicked, and he slid the guns to the door. Andy's mouth hung open.

"It's over. We couldn't win this one." Andy frantically disarmed himself as Merrill stepped closer to the door.

"We are unarmed." Merrill shouted. "We are giving up. I'm opening the door now." Merrill's hands shook as he took hold of the wooden bolt. The plank clapped as it hit the ground. Merrill shoved the door open and shaded his eyes as the light swam in. The sheriff and his deputy were pointing their rifles at him. He looked around the street. There wasn't a soul to be seen. He weakly raised his arms as they brought him to the ground. They saw Andy's wound and took him to the sheriff's office on foot.

Zeke being a large man made his corpse difficult to carry. They took his body to the edge of town and dumped it in a ditch. Nobody complained. The hearing and sentencing for the McClellan brothers were short and timely. The judge called for me soon after the sheriff had locked them in their cell.

"The two of you have been convicted of armed robbery, kidnapping, and accessory to murder, as well as the murder of a deputy," the judge started. Merrill and Andy stood up straight. The prosecutor played with his thumbs and had a glint in his eye.

"Merrill McClellan," the judge stated. "You will be sentenced to prison for fifteen years for all of the crimes mentioned, except for murder." The judge ceased his ruling with the clap of a gavel.

Merrill sat down and whispered to the appointed defense lawyer.

"Andrew Jorgenson," the judge barked. "You will be sentenced to death by hanging for the murder of Deputy Herald Sharpe. The execution will take place in two days." The gavel cracked, and the sound rippled across the room. Andy sat down with his head held low. Merrill's lip quivered as his ribs tightened. He stood; he had to stand.

"Your honor," he said. The judge gave him a shocked and curious look. "This was my idea, and I deserve to suffer the consequences of my friend. I won't let him go alone," he said with a gulp. He didn't look at Andy. He faced his judgment on his own.

Two days after the trial, I assumed my post at the top of the gallows. I remember Andy's trembling hands, as he needed help climbing to his death. Merrill stood proud and tall, looking at me with assurance behind his eyes. He turned sharply in front of me and stood at his post on the gallows. Before the masks were laid, they had some brief words to say.

"I'm sorry for what I did," Andy admitted. "I

wish I could take it back."

Merrill watched Andy one last time before staring at the crowd.

"Like I said in court," Merrill started. "This was my idea. I should have made a different plan for us. I do apologize."

The judge mentioned that it was merciful to the thief called Andy because his leg would become gangrened sooner or later. I didn't think much of it. They were brothers that hanged together.

## *The Hanging of the Law*

In Wind City, the sheriff and his deputy took great pride in their work. The pair was teamed up five years before I was called, and in the ten square acres of that town, hardly was a scream heard. Because of that, and the town's unspoken history, the sheriff and his deputy were glad for what they had done.

As a part of that unmentionable history, anyone with a bottle would be thrown in a cell at the sheriff's office. One of the last remnants of the booze-swigging days was Turner's Saloon. They didn't sell whiskey or beer there, and Turner covered the sign with a plank of wood that read "Casino". Every window in the place had been broken out at least once. There were as many as three previous owners before Turner, but he was the last one holding the bag. When he had to sell his beer and spirits wholesale to another saloon in the next town, he'd sobbed his way back to an empty shell of a place.

All he'd had left were some coins and dollars in the register, his safe, and three decks of cards on his nightstand. Since the sheriff and the mayor hadn't made that a crime, he found a new way to keep a roof over his head. Without libations, the cowboys stopped coming. There were fewer and fewer travelers coming to Wind City, and hardly anybody wanted to gamble while clinging for warmth next to the gray mountains.

Turner was stout and had a rouge complexion from his drinking days. His mustache lay flat; he couldn't afford the wax to pick it up anymore. On winter days, he would think about burning some of the furniture to stay warm at night. Instead, he just bought cloth and wool to fill up the draughts throughout his casino.

One card player stayed the night at Turner's. He lay in front of the fireplace and woke as stiff as a board. He brushed the sawdust and snow off his back. The cold white light shone through the windows and led him to the bar.

His old back and mangy beard ached. He stroked them both and waited for the man of the house to keep him company. The thin, persistent chill in the room put him in an ornery, desperate mood. He was hoping that Turner had gone to get some more firewood, but another visitor walked through the door.

"Where's Turner?" the visitor asked.

"I thought he went out. He must be asleep, sheriff."

The sheriff didn't believe that. He walked to one of the back doors, looking back at the old fool at the bar. He knocked politely.

"Open up, Turner. I need a word with you."

There was no answer, not even a stir.

"He might not wake up for some time, on account of…" He caught his tongue.

"Mr. Gimbal, were you here all night?"

"No, sir I came back for some morning coffee," he said with a chuckle. The sheriff's glare made him know that he shouldn't have. "Yes, I was here the whole night."

"Was it just you and Turner here?"

"No, there was one other."

"Who was it?" Gimbal wiped his nose and plucked at his beard. He turned away. The sheriff waited. Gimbal hoped he could hide in front of the sheriff's eyes, but they never left their place. Gimbal knocked the bar with his knuckle.

"Confound it," he muttered.

"What was that?"

"I'll tell you," he whispered. He waved the sheriff to come closer. He didn't move. Annoyed but not surprised, Gimbal faced the sheriff. "There was one other."

"Do you know his name?"

"No, but I know he's a soothsayer. I mean he could play the cards the way he wanted to play them. If he wanted you to win, he'd let you. If he wanted you to lose on his bluff, he'd force you. I lost a lot to him and Turner."

"Does Turner join in on card games these days?"

"There were only three of us, so he had to play. He didn't mind taking my money either."

"You know how gambling works. You can't always win."

"I know, but I think that fella was a cheat. He always had a look in his eye like he knew what would happen. I even told him he couldn't deal anymore, and he still won."

The Sheriff glanced around. "That's a shame, but I should let you know why I'm here. I got word that there's been whiskey moving through this casino. Is there anything you'd like to tell me, Mr. Gimbal?"

Gimbal remained silent.

The sheriff marched closer and his hand stretched over the bar. He grew taller next to Gimbal. He knew there was only one way out. The sheriff saw it in his eyes.

"I'll tell you, I'll tell you," he begged.

The sheriff's wolfish smile spread from ear to ear. "Well go on then."

"That fella that played me in cards, he is bringing in some tonight. They had a meeting about it. Afterwards they wanted to play a few games, so I agreed."

"Did you hear how much was coming in?"

"A cart load," Gimbal whispered. "He said he was going to bring a cart into town tomorrow."

"How many will be with him?"

"I'm not sure. He could be alone."

The door opened behind the sheriff. Turner held the back of his aching head. His eyes were cool and didn't treat the sheriff with any reverence.

"What is it, Owens?"

"It's...it's about your debts, Turner," the sheriff lied. "Mr. Henderson at the general store said that you've owed him for too long. I'm here to collect the money or take you to jail. Which is it going to be?"

"Keep your trousers on," Turner said. He did a slow about-face. He shuffled back inside his private quarters. The sheriff waited. He clicked his spurs on the floor. They spun around with the sound of a tiny wind chime. Turner's expression upon reentering the casino was not content. Owens thought the man might fall to his knees and be sick. Turner held onto the bar with all his might, doubled over like he was being twisted. The sheriff approached the man and took the money. He counted it.

"You still owe another dollar and eighteen cents, Mr. Turner."

Turner threw the nearest stool to the side. The sheriff swapped the cash between his hands and kept his right at the ready. Turner whirled around the bar to reach the register. He slapped the remaining sum onto the bar and looked at the sheriff with grinding teeth.

"Now, leave my shop." Owens took a look at the money and swept it into a pile.

"Thank you," the sheriff said with a tip of his hat. His spurs clanged along as he strolled out. Turner's eyes kept watching him, until they finally discovered Gimbal.

"Leave my shop. Now!" Gimbal moved like the

wind. The door didn't make any noise as he saw himself out. With a throbbing head, Turner told himself to put the past behind him.

That night, Owens and his deputy were playing a hand of cards. The deputy was a strong jawed and clean-shaven man. His blonde hair crept out of his hat. He grimaced as he made his move. The sheriff slapped his cards onto the table.

"Aw shoot," the deputy said. "You saw that a mile away, didn't you?"

"I just made the right move at the right time, Phillips."

"No, I made the wrong move at the right time for you."

"That may be," he looked at the cards.

Phillips stood up. "I'll be in the outhouse until tomorrow morning, just holler if you need me," The deputy let the last of his coffee run past his teeth. He pushed through the back door. A soft sound came from outside and a lantern started to glow.

Owens chewed over his coffee. He walked to the rear door, like he did every so often. He would look out the door, down Main Street. He looked as far as he could in the darkness, but they caught on something. His eyes widened and he snapped into a sprint. The soft howl of midnight in winter wrapped the empty sheriff's office.

The sheriff's feet plunged through the snow and carried him without restraint. He kept his eyes on the end of the street. The wind was freezing his eyes as dew hung on the corners. The lantern in his hand helped his feet find ground. Lights glowed inside Turner's Casino. As soon as he reached it, he placed his lantern at the door and retrieved his revolver.

Without a moment's hesitation, Owens threw open the door and aimed his revolver inside. Two men were placing the last of the crates in the casino. Bottles and bottles were stacked and stowed around the bar. Turner was quick to turn pale, and the other knew to run for his life, not that he showed any fear of losing it. The sly character crossed the casino and escaped out the rear door. Turner reached for the small shotgun that he had chained to his waist.

The sheriff nearly jumped out of his skin as Turner blew a hole in the wall next to him. The sheriff dove for a wooden pillar and sunk to the ground. Another blast rang out, and the pillar popped from the shot spraying across the oak. His hand plucked out the discharged shells and replaced them. Owens didn't give him a chance to ready his weapon.

One bullet ripped through Turner's gut. The shotgun flew out and hit his leg with the swing of the chain. The second bullet took off Turner's little finger before striking him in the heart.

Owens ran out for his lantern and threw himself towards the edge of the building. Around the corner, he saw the cart that Gimbal had promised. There was a snap of a whip, and the horses moved forward.

"Stop!" The sheriff shouted. He stood out in the open to take a better look, leaving himself exposed. The driver of the cart whirled around and fired at him. The bullet ricocheted off the lantern and ran through his elbow. The sheriff held his tongue between his teeth and screamed instinctively. Warm blood was starting to run through his sleeve. He lost his pistol in the snow and began to dig. Once his throbbing fingers found the familiar curve of the gun, he fired after the phantoms in the darkness.

Owens hobbled back to his office and kicked in the door. He shuffled inside, groaning like a wild animal. He held the sleeve of his wounded arm and tried to keep it in place. He sat hard on a chair and his wound grazed against his desk. He cried out in agony like a slaughtered pig. Half of his arm was covered in blood.

He plucked the knife out of his boot and

cautiously carved the sleeve of his coat and shirt from his arm. He examined the wound the best he could. The lamplight wasn't very good, and every twist sent a bolt of pain through him. His opened elbow shone in the light. The blood had stopped running, and his elbow was missing a piece. The stiff limb couldn't do much after suffering that kind of damage. The way it looked in that light was haunting. He was shocked and frightened by its grotesque appearance. He lost time while staring at it. Men have always found violence fascinating, like the flux of a flame.

There was a humming from outside. The doctor and a neighbor pushed through the door.

"Do you have a pail of water in here, sheriff?" the doctor asked, looking around.

"In the cell, I knew that would come in handy, not like this, of course." The doctor was already back with the water and raised the pail over his arm.

"Are you ready, sheriff?" he asked.

"Ready as ever," he said. The neighbor anticipated that this was not something he wanted to see.

"Do you need my help, doctor?" he offered.

"No, Dale, you've helped enough. I have everything I need." His eyes flashed intently to the wound. Dale stepped out as he saw the edge of the pail tip over. The doctor tried to be gentle. His patient howled and stomped his feet. His teeth almost cracked under the pressure, and foam started to reach the edges of his mouth. The doctor stopped pouring and wiped the blood away with his hands. He brooded over the wound. After a few moments, he looked intently at the sheriff.

"It's going to get infected. You don't want the gangrene. It's a nasty disease. I know that this won't be easy as you are the sheriff, but that arm is not fit for purpose any longer."

"What are you saying, doctor?" The sheriff said.

"The arm will need to be removed. From above the elbow," the doctor prescribed.

"My arm ain't coming off, doc."

"It will become infected if it doesn't, and you may die."

"How long do I have before it gets infected?"

"It could be tomorrow, or if you're lucky it could be a few days. I wouldn't take that risk if I were you, sheriff. We rely on you."

"Then we better pray for more time. This arm isn't coming off until I hunt down that man." He stood and walked to the cell. The patient took a bed and collapsed from exhaustion.

The morning snow lit up the town with a calm, placid grace. The sheriff took in the cool, brisk air before he decided to investigate the scene once more. Turner's corpse was unmoved. Nothing was touched in that building. There was something else that didn't move from the scene as well. When the shootout was taken outside, the sheriff fired into the darkness. The snow and clouded sky had shown that he had hit his mark.

The carriage had tipped over as the driver took it away from the road. The boulder it crashed into was bare of snow. One of the rear carriage wheels had broken in two, leading it to crash. Owens approached it, seeing the finer details lay out in the white expanse. The driver was killed. His head had dashed across a rock. Before his demise, he bled from a wound in his back. The horse tied to the carriage had frozen to death. Its nostrils were nearly frozen shut, and its hide was as cold as ice water. The sheriff stared at the horse. His lame hand brushed its crusted mane. His knuckles didn't bend; his fingertips scratched the surface.

He looked out toward the mountains. The marks of a horse's hooves were plain to see. His pained arm grew cold in the winter wind. He pondered the doctor's warning and wondered how far he could follow those tracks before sundown.

At the sheriff's office, Owens started to tie his saddle to his horse. The doctor watched him struggle. He seemed too proud to stop. Being out of breath from the now arduous task, he looked at the doctor with a disappointed expression.

"He won't come back," the doctor said. "There's no point in going after him in your condition."

The sheriff sighed deeply. His gaze brushed over the doctor's cautious face. "There is a point. When you start something, you need to finish it." He turned back to the empty main street. He cherished the sight of it, its memories. He thought it could be the last time he saw it. "This town needs to know that I fought for them," he said. "By getting rid of another criminal who might cause more harm. That's my job, it's my life's work."

"He's not coming back to Wind City. That's for sure," the doctor implored.

Owens turned back to his saddlebags. He shoved the rifle into its holster. His wound stung again. How was he going to use that rifle with one hand?

"Doc, I need you to get a message to the marshals. Tell them to follow those tracks by the carriage. Somebody needs to catch this man if I can't do it." A smile blew away from the doctor's face as Owens climbed onto his horse. The sheriff was determined to find the man, even if it killed him.

In the brutal cold of the mountains, the sheriff's palms started to slip with sweat. His vision grew clearer. Risk was possible. His man could be anywhere. He would have to rely on instinct, and he needed to be quick. His hair stood up and froze him to the bone. He was accustomed to law and order, now he was chasing after a deadly criminal. Owens cherished every moment he had left in those mountains.

Following the tracks, Owens knew that his man rode through the night. He didn't know how this fugitive could have done it without freezing to death. He must have stopped somewhere, deeper into the mountains. He climbed higher and higher into the sky piercing rocks that overlooked his county. The wind started to die down, and he could smell the pines. He could smell fire.

He's here, the sheriff thought. *He's near, somewhere.* He approached a plateau and could see a faint plume of smoke on the other side. He leaned closer to his horse's neck, staying low and watching carefully.

As he crested the hill, Owens saw a small fire and a horse standing in the open. His hand moved forward and drew his revolver. His eyes whipped around and he listened for any human sound. His feverish search came to an end with a bang. In all the excitement, he forgot where he was, but he recognized the one firing. Phillips was hiding, aiming for his next shot.

His deputy fired his revolver from the edge of the cliff. He had a foothold near the edge and had the cover of the elevation. His head and shoulder popped up above the surface to fire another round. Owens turned his horse to the side as he fired. The recoil was tough to handle, he felt off balance and couldn't hit his mark.

He had to make himself smaller and dismounted the horse. A bullet cracked and flew over his shoulder. He fell out of the saddle with a grunt. He hid behind the horse while searching for his enemy. The fear of death tightened around his throat. He looked at the spot where he last saw him.

Phillips was gone. Owens kept his revolver pointed there anyway. The dull hum from the guns stayed in the air, the smoke washed away with the wind. He held his horse firm and walked to the side, hoping to spot his foe. The snow sounded underneath his feet. The cold returned to his face.

Phillips leapt up and fired as he crawled to his feet. Owens fell back. He twisted and pulled himself up. He threw his chest forward, not wasting any time. Phillips went for his horse near the fire, but Owens was quick to pull the trigger. A crack and a visceral grunt filled the mountains. Phillips writhed in agony and held his leg.

"Don't move!" Owens roared. "I'll shoot if you reach for that gun!" He shuffled as quickly as he could to the wounded, growling Phillips. He never let him out of his sight.

The deputy looked at his leg in unshakeable pain. His cries had died down, but his face was wracked with despair.

"You can't get away now," Owens declared. "Are you proud of yourself?" He asked. His partner groaned, not thinking of him. "Look at me!"

Phillips' head snapped upward. He wasn't impressed.

"What's the next part of your plan?" Phillips asked. His laugh drew fiery anger within Owens. His mockery led the sheriff's boot to strike his shoulder. He fell over with a startled grunt.

"There isn't anything funny about what just

happened."

"I know that. It was all very serious business." His cavalier mood stunned the sheriff. "How long do you think you have to get back to town? Can you get back by sunset?"

Owens examined Phillips' face. Where had the man he knew gone?

"I know I should have left earlier," Phillips muttered.

"You shouldn't have left at all. You almost killed me."

"Then you wouldn't be sheriff of this piss pot county anymore. What would be so bad about that?"

"You swore an oath."

"Oaths don't matter," he sighed.

"That's why you're here, and it's because of that oath that I'm here with you. I could have let you go."

"You still can." His conceited demeanor never left, even when his partner's revolver hung over him.

"I treated you like a brother. Now, we're like Cain and Abel," he seethed.

"Only if you kill me." Chuckles escaped from his mouth.

Maybe he was drunk. How could he know this man? He was a stranger. Owens' shoulders sank. He extended his hand, and Phillips took it. Two lame men helped each other onto the horse. Owens pushed as Phillips hopped on and climbed over. Phillips' blood ran down the horse's flanks. Owens never looked back in case Phillips tried to escape or reach for his revolver. His horse carried them back down the mountain.

When I heard the story, I thought of that choice: to let the man who nearly killed you escape death for a few more days. Naturally, I thought about what I would have done. Is there any difference between a sheriff killing and a hangman hanging? I imagined a rifle kicking against my shoulder, leaving that grinning villain in the snow. Then I thought of my father, the blast rattling in my chest. Perhaps it was best to leave it to the judges. Then I thought of the corrupt ones who made me kill all the same.

The sheriff watched from the small crowd, missing an arm. Why wait when you've lost so much? A dull cloud filled my mind, and the deputy met his justice.

## The Hanging of a Deserter

Danglars thought that Fort Washakie was a ramshackle barracks with rotting walls. He had a lot of time to make that observation as he watched over his men. He would stand guard at night on the parapets. On his first night at the fort, he thought that he had been slighted. It felt like a demotion without the usual display of shame and dishonor. He was sent out into the wilderness.

The men were weary of war. They had skirmishes in the mountains with the Cheyenne. They weren't green by any means, but Danglars was not satisfied. Their wild beards and torn uniforms seemed like an act of sedition against him personally. He thought of having the men shave, but the cold winter air made him think twice.

The men started to feel at ease with Danglars once he'd lead them into battle.

"There he goes!" Danglars shouted from his horse. He whipped the animal and chased after an Indian brave. His twenty men made a thunderous charge after him. The sounds ricocheted off the mountains. They dove deeper into the wilderness, unknowingly following the brave to his war party.

Danglars and his men rode until a clearing opened before them. Danglars halted his horse; its head writhed, misting from the nose. His men closed in on his flanks. A small echo grew and grew along the towering rocks. The brave reached his war party at the edge of the clearing. He turned and lowered himself alongside his brothers, waiting in preparation.

"Dismount! Now!" Danglars shouted.

The men dismounted and crouched.

"Circle the horses! Stay close to one another!"

A mix of legs formed a pacing whirlwind in the fallen snow. The men cast their eyes around the clearing and the mountains. Danglars and his horse filled the middle of the circle and watched the line of trees. The painted Indians were waiting; they hoped for a mistake. Their heads moved like shadows under the shade of the pines. They were thinking, which meant *he* had time to think too.

"Arm yourselves, men. Be ready for the first arrow; don't let them cause you to panic. We need to use as much cover as we can. Have you seen any above us?"

The horses snorted as they uprooted the snow.

"No, sir," a soldier said finally.

Danglars looked behind the men; there was nothing.

"Let us distance ourselves, men. The closer to the path we are, the quicker our escape." He pulled on his horse's reins. It stepped back as the others led their creatures further away from the trees.

A silent flight of arrows plunged down on them. The sight nearly stunned Danglars. Horses roared and slipped from their masters' clutches. The men in the front of the circle reached for their weapons and began to fire into the forest.

Danglars wrenched his horse forward. His revolver hung heavy in his hand. The braves were too far for him to fire. His horse dug its hooves in behind him. He leaned forward, trying to reach his men. Another swarm of arrows flew at them. More came in single zips.

"Move those horses forward, these men need shelter!" Danglars shouted, waving his arm forward.

An arrow forced itself into the breastplate of his horse. It jolted back and forth, unleashing its horrid cry. Danglars lined up his horse with the men and leapt on top of it to keep it from running off. Its legs folded, and he could hear its lungs begin to fill with blood. Its breathing crackled through all the sounds of chaos. Danglars held the horses head upright to keep its back as high as possible. Two soldiers were lying prone, firing at the enemy.

"Come here!" Danglars shouted. "Fire behind here!"

The men crawled on hand and foot. He held the horse still; its breathing came with long pauses. The men fired from the top of its back, sliding behind it when they needed to replenish their ammunition. Danglars looked around in terror. The men were firing blindly at their foes while desperately holding onto their horses. He turned to face the enemy and fired from the body of his animal companion. More arrows snapped against the ground and drilled into men's limbs.

"Fall in here!" Danglars roared. "Bring your horses over! We need a line of defense! Right here!"

He sat behind his horse's head and began reloading his revolver. The taxing practice wasted more time than he could afford as his men were falling all around him. Some wounded and untouched men laid their horses down alongside Danglars.

"Sir, what are your orders?" A soldier shouted over the gunfire.

"Hold this position with all your might! How many horses do we have?" He went back to loading his revolver.

"Four, sir!"

"What about the others? Are they dead or did they run away?" Danglars asked without taking his eyes off his weapon.

"Some dead, some ran off, sir!"

"Keep firing!" He growled to the others. "Don't let them get away!"

Then came yips and bellows from the trees. Two dozen Indians appeared from the darkness of the pines. Horsemen and braves on foot charged the soldiers with axes held high. Danglars looked the first in the eye and discharged his weapon before the axe could reach him. The man's corpse flew from his horse's back, and the animal reared in terror. The other soldiers fired at the braves on horseback. More of the Indians followed as they saw their brothers fall.

"Fire every bullet you have left!" Danglars ordered. He picked off the closest of the charging braves. They sprinted at the trench of dead horses without fear. Danglars yelled from the depths of his soul and stepped forward with sabre drawn. One Indian saw Danglars as he ran and gritted his teeth for a blow with his club. Danglars pressed forward and ran the man through. Another was nearly on top of him and he swiped to and fro. Feeling the uncontrolled strength of another man frightened Danglars and steeled his spirit. His eyes were vigilant and watched his enemy's weapon parry his attacks.

A great roar from his men followed him and clashed with the enemies'. Rifles cracked from firing bullets and bludgeoning men without mercy. They used the leverage they could to slice another inch from their foe. Biting and punching to free their hand was common. Blinding with knives and swift cuts into the centers of men made the clearing howl with agony. When Danglars freed himself of a living enemy, he pounced on the nearest that threatened his men.

The clatter and screams of battle fell into the cold silence. Danglars looked at his comrades and adversaries lying in the bloodstained snow. They could hear each other's hearts pounding, hoping that was the end of it all. There were no more arrows being loosed, no more knives driving into flesh.

"How many do we have left?" Danglars asked.

"Eight, sir, two are wounded," a soldier reported.

"What about these horses?"

"Four, sir," he said with a sunken heart.

"That's not enough. Can you ride?" He asked the pair of wounded soldiers.

"I can, sir," one said, rising to his feet. The other stiffly joined him.

"I can too, sir," said the other.

"Bring their bodies, the two of you can ride. The rest of us will walk."

"No, sir," the wounded soldiers insisted. "We can't ride while the others walk, sir."

"I gave you an order, men," he said tenderly. "Do as you're told." Danglars took a corpse by the shoulder and hoisted it up. The men snapped into action.

The journey to the fort was a solemn one. Their frozen feet trudged through snow. The dark stains on their uniforms imbued black moods over them. The dark parade did not return to the fort until the sun had set. The small flames of the lanterns and fires around the walls could be seen in the faint light. The fires were guiding lights rather than sources of warmth. They were tokens, trinkets to men and corpses who were nearly frozen through.

The men started to love Danglars, either by bleeding with him in battle or by the legend of his ferocity. He could feel their respect in their smiles and focused acknowledgement as he spoke to them. They all rose to attention the moment he entered the barracks, something that he was not accustomed to at his last post. Danglars did not fall into complacency with this newfound admiration. He still roamed the walls of the fort at night to watch over his men.

His footsteps knocked across the planks of the parapets. His nightly watch was calming. The air constricted around him, but he embraced the cold. The pitch-black night hid its secrets, and only few were illuminated by the blaze of the torches. His eyes wandered the shallow, visible expanse beyond the fort's walls. Some snow began to fall, and the wind emerged from the darkness.

He pointed his torch outward. Seeing nothing, he thought to see how the other sentries were keeping warm. Something appeared from the corner of his eye, a distinct white mark in a sea of pitch. He waved his torch to the sight and saw a pale man, a ghost.

The ghost of an Indian brave stood before him with shoulders back and eyes narrowed.

Danglars brandished his torch to frighten the man. The ghost moved closer. He did not walk; he simply appeared closer to the wall. Danglars' eyes grew wide, and his throat begged to let out a scream, but the brave was already at the wall, climbing, digging his nails and knife into the wood.

Danglars threw his coat open to reach for his revolver. His freezing fingers fumbled for it. With his eyes off the brave, he heard a voice in Cheyenne. He couldn't grasp it. A curse? A warning? He shoved his revolver forward. The ghost stood at the end of the barrel. His chest, unmoving, and eyes were square with his. Danglars wondered in that moment if he recognized him. It might have been one of the men he had killed that day. Not a sound could be heard over the gunfire and his own bitter screams.

One of the sergeants sprang to his feet from the barracks. He saw that two sentries were approaching a frantic Captain Danglars. Danglars' weapon was drawn at the men, trembling in hysteria. They walked towards him, spoke softly, and extended their palms to him. Danglars' eyes shot around the parapet. He had to see the ghost again to know where he was. Expecting a knife in the back or another charge, he whipped his head around to find him.

The men still moved in closer. Danglars saw them and felt trapped. They didn't know where the Indian was. He had to protect them. The pale specter appeared again. He was behind them with his knife drawn and bellowing a silent cry. Danglars fired behind his men, over their shoulders until his weapon was silent.

The sergeant took Danglars by the shoulders and tackled him to the ground. They dragged him away. The heels of his boots were raw and two trails in the snow followed him. Danglars muttered into the night. When they locked him in the cell, the surgeon took out a bullet from a sentry's shoulder. Their brave leader had fallen, and a stranger took his stead inside a cell.

The decision was made. He would be executed for endangering the men. A new captain would be brought to the fort along with more reinforcements to break the rest of the Cheyenne war parties in the mountains. Captain Danglars' legacy would be wiped clean for an even bigger plan. His men had their orders.

Danglars, weak and cold in his cell, was awakened by

the creaking of his cage. Two soldiers took him by the arms. He had no strength to walk. His senseless feet were dragged across the ground to the courtyard of the fort. The men threw him against a post and tied his hands tightly around it. He swayed his limbs and back, but his restraints were taut against the pole. The sergeant, who found him in that state, stood at the side with his sword in hand.

Three men were chosen, and they stood at attention in front of him. Danglars awoke from his exhausted frenzy to see the men he had fought alongside in front of him, now his executioners. Their expressions were complex. Each had a different one from the last, and they changed when they looked away from their captain.

"Present arms!" The sergeant's bark caused the men to shudder. The sword rose to the clearing sky. "Take aim!"

The end was coming. Danglars could not run. The ghost of the Indian brave was floating past their shoulders. Danglars was certain of it. He couldn't get a good look; he was too quick for his eyes to see.

"Fire!" Danglars' back stretched against the pole. Cold air fell from his lungs. He breathed. He could breathe. The sergeant was shouting at the men, wishing unspeakable things on each of them.

Danglars wasn't sure why he was alive.

"We fought with him in the mountains, sergeant. He's a good man. Let him be discharged."

"Those are not your orders, private! I will discharge you if you do not execute this man. Do I need to tell you again how much of a threat he is to these men?"

"No, sergeant," he said, defeated.

"Fall in line!" The sword cut through the air. The men aimed their rifles again. "Fire!" One bullet was fired. It struck the wall of the fort.

"I won't do it, sergeant." One soldier stepped forward. Another followed.

"This isn't fair, sergeant. We can't kill him."

"You're all facing a court martial when this is over. I need three volunteers." His eyes swept across the men's faces. He paced across the courtyard. His intimidating gaze didn't force anyone forward.

"He lost his mind," said the wounded sentry. "He can't help it. This isn't right."

"Dammit, men!" The sergeant's roar emptied the fort of sound. "If you think insubordination is going to become commonplace, there will be hell to pay!" He turned and marched back to the barracks. The others looked around. The wind started to lift and cool the air. The two men who had taken Danglars from his cell untied him and placed him back inside.

The day I came to the fort the men wore morose expressions. They were ordered to give aid to my construction of the gallows. They stood by. The sergeant made it clear that the gallows would be permanent. The gray winter days passed by. The fire inside the barracks held no warmth, and the food had no taste. The time I spent there was torturous.

Standing on the gallows, I saw the beloved captain. His feet were dragged through the snow and his clothes no longer fit. His sunken cheeks and pale face were haunting. His head hung low until he faced me. His face became animated with life but not the life that any man would want to live. His eyes were shocked. His head rocked and twisted. What was left of that captain was nothing his men could recognize. He was a frenzied dog. He shivered throughout the ceremony. The ordeal made my hands shake too. Once I tapped my fingers against the lever, they stopped in their quake. Another lost man on the frontier of civilization.

## *The Hanging of a Madman*

After the hanging of Captain Danglars, I thought of how it must have felt to lose one's mind. Seeing ghosts wherever you looked, always glancing over your shoulder. I felt that in my own way. I wondered if I would be visited by ghosts of the men I hanged. In the weak light of dawn, I dreamt of those pale figures with familiar faces. This did not frighten me. Their eyes held their stories. I thought about each hanging, they deserved punishment, I knew. I looked into their faces. They pitied me. They pitied me. *What have I done wrong?*

My heavy arms pushed beyond them, like wading through water. I searched for my father's face on his final day. Did he want this for me? *What should I do?* Then a building cloud emerged in my memory. I wanted to forget, but I knew I ought to remember. My mind and soul began to whirl, restless and seeking absolution, comfort—peace. I woke with the clear memory of the madman.

The rotting door of an abandoned shack creaked open, revealing bloodied floorboards. Besides the light shining from the open front door, the house seemed to keep the sun out completely. Marshal Hightower's spurs clicked and rattled as he entered the dark dwelling. His eyes caught every corner of the house. There was no movement. He could hear his heartbeat bounce off the low ceiling beams as they echoed throughout the house. His horse flicked its tail. There was nothing inside.

His partner was sitting on top of a horse, patiently waiting for the next order. Hightower looked around the front of the house and wiggled his mustache, trying to sense anything he could, anything he might have missed.

"Take my horse back to the stream. Go back into town and come back with some more men, just in case."

"That'll be hours, we might not reach you until sundown."

"You better hurry then." Hightower patted his horse on the neck. His partner steered their horses away, disappearing between crowded pines. Hightower shut the door to escape the summer heat. He took another look at the house. The windows were frail, cracked, and broken. There only a bed in one room, and the kitchen was bare with unhinged cupboards exhibiting their emptiness. Hightower checked to see if there was a back door and slid his feet across the ground, looking for a hidden cellar. He found a back door, but there was no secret latch.

Hightower positioned himself the best he could. He took a small chair and pressed it into a corner. He could see the front door clearly, and there wasn't much room between the back door and his line of sight. Waiting is a serious game. Seemingly, like idleness, waiting grows on the senses, making one desperate for excitement. Hightower didn't want to be tempted by looking at his pocket watch, so he started a cigarette. After smoking about half of it, he rose from the chair and looked around in the bedroom. There weren't any cigarettes, cigars, or pipes anywhere. He snuffed out his cigarette and waited.

After hours of watching and listening, Hightower could take some joy in hearing the rustling of the pines in the wind. As the sun set, he felt his stomach drag inside him. He didn't know where his men were, and he didn't know when the resident of that shack was going to turn up.

In the dying light, he counted the bullets in his revolver. All six were there. He placed them on the shelf next to him and played with them one at a time in his hand. The dull bluish gray light guided his fingers as they placed each round in their chamber. He snapped it back in place and sighed. Even that couldn't take his mind off of the task at hand.

With what little light was left, he aimed into the next room. He could hardly see the end of his revolver. It was guesswork as he waited in the darkness, and all that time he had hoped that his partner would return. They're lost, he thought. The wind was starting to chill him to the bone. He crossed his arms and began to shake.

After some immeasurable time had passed, he heard something. A twig snapped. His eyes widened. His revolver wasn't ready to fire, and neither was he. He couldn't see. He couldn't tell an armoire from a shadow in that dark house. The back door creaked and slapped shut. Two feet swept against the ground. He heard shuffling and the quick start of a match. The next room lit up with lantern light. Hightower waved his revolver over, ready. A short, thick bearded man with a rifle on one shoulder and two rabbits on the other turned to face him with the lantern held high.

"US Marshal."

The man didn't say anything, didn't move.

"You were spotted fleeing the McFarland house. You'll be coming with me."

The man never moved when he saw the marshal. Hightower slowly rose to his feet, keeping his eyes focused on his captive. He motioned the man towards him. The bearded man walked closer. His eyes never moved, fixed on Hightower's face.

"Go out the front door," Hightower said.

The man, clearly scared, turned and marched out. The marshal kept his gun close to the man's back. Stepping out onto the porch, Hightower stopped him. He peeled the rifle from his shoulder and threw the rabbit carcasses on the ground. There weren't any white horses in the darkness.

"Move forward," Hightower said. More trees appeared in the light. He cavalierly fired three bullets into the air.

The prisoner doubled over and held his ears.

"Stokes! Stokes, over here!" Hightower bellowed into the air. When the echoes faded and the trees whistled again, they heard horses snort and trot towards them. Hightower placed the hot barrel against his prisoner's neck. He squealed and threw his head wildly.

Stokes kicked his horse through the pines and shined his light on the men. Five other deputies on white horses came into the light.

"You're under arrest for suspicion of murder." The marshal quickly tied rope around the man's hands and shoved him forward to Stokes' horse, lifting him over the side. Stokes smiled, knowing that it was a long, uneven ride back to town.

The door to the local jail was enthusiastically thrown open. The suspect was summarily dragged to a cell and pushed onto the bed. Hightower and Stokes stood outside of the cage, watching the hairy, feral beast.

"Do you want to start questioning him now?" Stokes asked Hightower.

"Give me some time alone with him. I'll get it out of him." Stokes followed the other deputies out of the room. Hightower's steps rang dull and filled every cell. He took a stool and a nearly extinguished candle over to the prisoner. He slapped the stool onto the floor and lit the candle before setting it between them. Hightower began writing notes for the record.

"Name?" He asked. The light flickered in the man's eyes at the dark corner of the cell. He hesitated to answer.

"Gillman," he said.

Hightower wrote that down and decided to push on. "A neighbor of the McFarland's said that he saw you run from their house. He said that you were carrying a knife. He saw you strike the McFarland girl in the back not too far from their home." A twisted ankle under a white dress imprinted in his mind. The crimson flashed over her pale back. Her eyes stretched open, hoping to see more of life. He looked into the dark cell. "Do you have anything to say?"

Gillman didn't speak.

"Will you deny it?"

"No," the prisoner allowed to leave his lips.

"I will take that as a confession," Hightower said. He stood and placed the notebook in his pocket.

"I won't confess."

Hightower stopped himself and lowered his eyes,

looking into the cell again. "Because you didn't do it?"

"It felt…" Gillman looked down and brushed his arms. "How...how many people have gone missing in this county, Marshal?"

"Four since the snow melted." Gillman gathered his thoughts, breathed.

"I'll tell you where I left them, but you'll have to listen first."

Hightower's face twisted in anger. His red cheeks blazed hotter than the candle at his feet.

"Who was the first one?" Gillman asked.

Hightower sat on the stool.

"Who was the first one?" He asked again.

"A trapper who lived in the hills… Bruce." Hightower said.

"Where did he live?"

"In that shack, I reckon."

"Very good, but can one say he was missing all the way out there? He was a difficult man to kill. He struck me onto the floor when I lanced him with my knife. I got the better of him. I took my beating, but I squirmed on top to press down on that knife. Who was the second?"

"Margaret Barnes," Hightower's tongue turned in his cheek.

"Washing," Gillman muttered. "I remember my reflection in the pond. She never saw me." A tear escaped his eye. "Cold...but I brought her down. Down with rocks," he remembered.

"Where?" Hightower projected. There was no sound from the cavernous, dark cell. He sighed and paged through his notebook.

"Helena Swarthout, she was seventeen."

"Blonde in the green," Gillman whispered. "She was an orb of yellow light, the only distinguishing figure in that sea of grass and trees. I think I could find her. But why did she have to scream? She screamed and screamed and screamed." Gillman covered his ears and dug into his scalp with his sharp nails.

"That's enough," Hightower groaned. "You will tell us where the bodies are, and then you will be brought to justice."

"You'll never find their bones!" Gillman shrieked. His lower lip shivered. "You won't find them without me. I want someone to listen. A man who has dealt with death before..."

Hightower searched Gillman's face. *How did he know?* It was easy enough to guess that a marshal would have killed before, but he knew. He could see the certainty in his eyes, clamped on his.

"Walter Burns, the farm hand who worked for the McFarlands."

"Mmm…" Gillman pressed his head against the wall. "I remember happening upon him in the hills. He was a handsome boy. Too dumb for his own good. I think the two of them were getting ready for a romantic escape. They may have been leaving for Nevada or California, or some place. He had two bags and a mule with him. The girl you found this morning was supposed to meet him at a secret hiding place. It wasn't out of sight of course. It was a clear-cut path; anybody could find it, and I found them." He inhaled indulgently.

"You know," he continued, "you might think people go out quietly, like a bird struck from the air or a deer shot in its side. No…no, he screamed. He screamed. He hollered, and I was shocked that she never heard him. I thought they would hear him throughout the valley. He didn't have much to say. He let out a little whimper, when he knew he had been beaten.

"I dragged his body back. It took some time. And that is when she saw me, lifting her bloody beloved on top of his mule. She screamed too. She tried to hide, but I could hear her heartbeat through the trees. You can hear everything in those hills, except for a cry for help. She nearly escaped too, out of the woods. She fell down the hill, snapping her ankle. And I tumbled down after her, a heart-pounding tumble. With grey skies lighting my way..."

"Enough!" Hightower roared. He looked deeper into the cell, casting a piercing gaze at the killer. "You've confessed to murder. You will be sentenced in a hearing tomorrow morning. The judge may give you leniency, but that's a small chance... What did they mean to you? Why would you do it?"

"There was no reason..." Hightower stirred in his seat.

"Did you do it to...hide what you did to them?"

"No, it was never like that. It was beyond that. Cheap. Nothing. Nothing hollow like that... It felt good. Transcendent above the rest..."

Hightower clutched the bars of the cell and rattled them. "You keep your twisted dreams to yourself. You're going to hell. You hear me?"

Gillman waited. He pondered and waited. He slid across the bed, closer to the bars. The candlelight exposed his rapturous face.

"Have you ever been tempted?" Gillman's eyes grew wet. His eyes reached out without moving a muscle.

The marshal rattled the bars again. He tried

tearing them apart in his grasp. The muscles recoiled against his bones, knowing they couldn't move mountains. He sighed deeply, and Gilman waited. He leaned closer again.

"Have you ever felt that fog…cloud around the corners of your eyes, making you feel like there's nothing else in the world besides what lies ahead of you? You've never wanted to do it, not really. But when you want to, when you won't deny yourself that pleasure, would you resist it? You're not better. You've never been tempted. And the only thing that separates us is that temptation."

Marshal Hightower left that room with dejected shoulders and an exhausted, hanging face. His eyes were gloomy and wet. The deputies asked him what had happened, and he never answered. His gaze didn't leave his feet or the ground they walked on.

The deputies carried Gillman to the places where he said the remains were left behind. Only one was buried. The others were left to decay in the open. Every participant of nature eroded them beyond recognition. When Gillman's day finally came, there was no pastor. The townsfolk didn't want him close to the murderer, the man who could not deny the pleasures of the flesh.

Marshal Hightower's eyes were dull, without their reflective glow. The edges of his eyes were painted red. When the gallows came into view, he pushed Gillman forward. He pushed him away to be rid of him. He hoped that each shove would be the last touch between him and that man. Gillman began to walk ahead quicker than Hightower's hand could reach. He marched up the scaffold, and the marshal watched with his lips apart.

Gillman's noose cracked and held tightly. Hightower's cheeks pulled back with relief, for a moment. Once the marshal was satisfied, his face turned dark. His cheeks grayed and he turned and went headlong into the corner saloon. They had to drag him out later that evening. Garbled words sprang out from his punch-stained mouth. They were half-sayings and twisted memories. His spurs dragged across the floor.

## *The Hanging of Justice*

I was called by official decree to Rock Springs. Something had happened there that caused quite a storm. The message lacked detail, but I knew I would learn soon enough. A battalion of the U.S. Cavalry was stationed there, and they'd asked for an executioner. I glumly accepted and bought the train ticket. I felt cold inside the train car. I knew there was something different about this summons. With that many soldiers preserving order in Rock Springs, there must have been some terrible act committed.

Rock Springs smelled rotten, worse than before. The air was damp, and the smoke from the town hung just over my head. It was like some desolate swamp. I watched my step as I placed my feet on the platform.

The military encampment was not difficult to find. They'd found a field where the sun shone. Looking back at Rock Springs, it seemed like a black spot on the green plains of the territory. A pair of General McConnell's soldiers escorted me to his tent. The tall, lean man with a large mustache seemed, on first impression, to be a civilized man, someone that we needed in parts like Rock Springs. Seeing those blue uniforms was comforting; they seemed to be a symbol of hope that day. General McConnell, looking me over, welcomed me to sit.

"So, you're the hangman," he asked.

"Yes, sir."

"We have a trial coming. It's a grave one, as you know."

"Yes, sir."

"I have seen a lot of bloodshed in my days. I have fought against Mexicans, Rebs, and Indians, but I haven't seen anything like this off the battlefield. There's been a massacre. There were two warring clans of sorts, and I think we know who started it. It's going to take a lot of rope to bring justice to this city."

"I understand, sir."

"Do you know how to ride?"

"I do, sir."

"Then come with me."

I followed him on horseback through Rock Springs. The yellow-eyed miners watched us trot by. Their coal-stained appearance made them hard to look at. You can't tell the guilty from the innocent by sight, but they all seemed to be marred by sin in a conspicuous way.

After leaving the Black Spot of the territory, we found the remains of the massacre. That rotten smell was that of flesh. The dull, white sunlight exposed it to man and God. Some of McConnell's men were starting to bury what they could. I placed the crook of my elbow over my nose.

"The Manchurians were hired to work in the mines," he said. "The white workers were organizing a strike for more pay. Then the mining company brought their replacements to town. There are more than a dozen dead, as you can see."

"What about the corpses? Why did no one bury them?"

"They were just working men. They brought no families with them."

"Couldn't somebody have buried them?"

"Nobody cared to," he said. He turned his horse around. I followed, keeping my eyes on the grisly sight. Returning to Rock Springs, with the knowledge of what evil deeds had been committed and left to be seen, I ground my teeth at seeing them walk free. How many did it? Which ones deserve it? Then a cold wave wiped across my brow, pondering. Justice would have to be found in court, not vigilante adventure.

The court and jury were assembled quickly at the behest of McConnell's battalion. His soldiers were guarding every entrance. They had two troopers flanking the judge, and two more each guarded the plaintiff and defendants. The other Manchurian workers sat behind the plaintiff, while the other white workers and their women and children sat behind the defendants. Others had arrived to witness the testimony. Some were reporters from Cheyenne; others were from as far as Chicago and New York.

"All rise!" A blue coat soldier bellowed. We stood to attention. The bald, sweating judge stepped from his office and took his place above the townspeople. He motioned for us to sit. He cleared his throat and wrung his hands, brooding over the case.

"Ladies and gentlemen, we are gathered today to hear the testimony and defense of an incident that happened in the Manchurian work camp. This incident resulted in the death of twenty-four workers as well as injuries to several others. We will first hear from the plaintiff."

The court was quiet. Every eye lifted with the plaintiff. He approached the witness box while struggling with a cane. When he turned to face the court, we could see the many bruises and cuts across the side of his face. If he were a workingman, he must not have eaten in days. His clothes hung over him like a coatrack.

"This is proof," he pointed to his bruises. "This is proof. The bodies out there is proof. They all did it. We were outnumbered. How this happen without big number?"

By the time he said this, the court was boiling in fury. The judge's gavel struck several times in order to regain control over the room.

"They were proud of it too. They go their bars and laughed about it. I know those men did it," his finger accused the defendants. "And many more did too."

"Order!" The judge cried over the hisses.

The plaintiff took his time to speak. He thought deeply. My eyes caught the chair where he'd sat before. The table was empty. There was no prosecution, nobody to represent him.

"Twenty dead and many more hurt…how you think happen?" His lips trembled, and his eyes sank to the ground.

The hardened hearts of the crowd gave no notice. The judge sent him back to his seat. He whispered to the other Manchurians in their language.

"The defense would like to remind your honor that a plaintiff needs a witness, not a simple accusation," the white men's lawyer scolded.

"Uh, right…" the judge cleared his throat. "Does the prosecution have any witnesses? Do you have anyone who saw the attack?" The plaintiff whispered to the others. One shot up and climbed over the partition. The plaintiff followed with his slow gait.

A soldier stopped the man before he reached the witness stand and made him place his hand on a Bible. The soldier began speaking, and the man looked over to the plaintiff. The plaintiff nodded. The witness did too. After swearing to tell the truth, the witness began giving his testimony. It became clear to everyone that he could not speak English. The plaintiff interpreted for the witness. Hearing enough, the defense lawyer rose to his feet.

"Objection, your honor! This court cannot confirm what the witness is saying. The plaintiff could be saying what he wants the witness to say."

"You're right," the judge said. "Do you have any other witnesses who can speak English?" The plaintiff was speechless. His witness asked for interpretation, but the plaintiff's mouth hung agape. The judge spoke to the witness and pointed him back to his seat. The witness hesitated and then returned to the other aggrieved Manchurian workers.

"We will hear a closing argument from the defense."

The plaintiff moved for the chosen defendant to make his speech. The barrel-chested, strong-jawed man stood in front of the court. His lungs heaved in to fill the room with his cutting voice.

"We are honest workingmen. We do not deserve to have our names thrown in the mud like this. It's all hearsay, isn't it? There wasn't any trouble before they showed up. We had a claim to that mine, because, from that mine, we earned the clothes on our backs and the roofs over our heads. And I say, and every man worth his salt should say, a man cannot be guilty of defending his livelihood," the defendant declared.

The court applauded thoroughly. The judge knocked on his desk with his fist. The court only brought themselves to silence when they chose to.

"Is there anything else you would like to say to the court?" The judge asked.

"I and every man you see seated at that table are free of guilt!" Another crash of applause came from the white workers.

"You may return to your seat," the judge said, only the man he spoke to could hear him over the din of the crowd. "The jury will convene in my quarters and come to a conclusion on the evidence provided." He and the jury retired to a back room while the Manchurians spoke amongst themselves. Their plaintiff's eyes were cast on the ground. After a quarter hour of deliberation, the judge and jury returned.

"The jury has reached a verdict," the judge claimed with a document in hand. "The defendants, Mr. Johnson, Mr. Swanson, Mr. Lundgaard, Mr. Olson, Mr. Lundqvist, and Mr. O'Leary have been found not guilty of this crime."

The white workers and their families hollered and gave a big hurrah for their guiltless gentlemen. The smell of bloated flesh and bare bone stung my nose, and I forced my way out of the courtroom.

Pushing through shoulders and elbows, I left the courtroom. The soft summer air was not pleasant to me. It seemed out of place. The workers and their families cheered and made a parade to the nearest saloon. There was nothing to build and no lives to take. I felt relieved but burdened. The jury had decided. Nobody would die. I felt that was unjust. I wasn't needed.

The general was smoking a pipe in his tent. His eyes were downcast at one of its corners. His gaze didn't break until I knocked on his desk. He was hoping it was one of his soldiers. He seemed like he needed to make some excuse, give an explanation for what I saw.

"This trial is unfair," I said. "We all know what happened. It was a brawl that left men dead in the open!"

"It was," he said.

"What are we going to do about it?"

"There is nothing *we* can do. The verdict has been decided." He smoked his pipe, disdaining defeat in calm silence. I waited for a sign there was some other scheme he had in mind. His glazed eyes stared off into the corner of his tent.

My hands fell to my side. I gave up. My jaw loosened, and my eyes never left his face. Not knowing how to proceed, he chose one of the keys from his pocket and placed it into a lock in one of the drawers. A few bank notes fell onto my side of the table. He spoke, but I just looked at them. He gave up speaking to me. The wind started to blow; the notes' edges started to flap. I took that as a sign that I should take my money while I could. It was easy to make, but I didn't know what to do or how to think.

On the train home, I thought. I thought about the souls of those twenty-four men. I thought about the souls of those whom I'd hanged. What would God do with them? Then I thought of the living. I thought I was supposed to be a force for justice. But I was just a tool for the capricious hearts of men.

I thought of running back to the courtroom and demanding the trial be fair and true. I imagined striking those guiltless men and being swallowed by the mob, broken and battered. Maybe that would count. The Manchurians didn't, not in court or anywhere near here.

I gave up. I felt like a coward admitting it, but I did. I took the train home and slept well. My conscience didn't matter. The case needed no second trial. It was done. It didn't count. I could kill, but I couldn't change the verdict. I couldn't move the world.

## *The Hanging of a Salesman*

After the Rock Springs trial, I didn't leave my home. I never spoke to another soul. My days consisted of working in the garden, feeling the sun on my cheeks. I drank more than I ate to tell the truth. The blurred sun wasn't as harsh, and the work was slow and easy thanks to the taskmaster.

I looked at the garden, measured all that I had, every tool, crop, and piece of timber, and I weighed my choices, whether I could leave my profession. Could I survive without payment, like a yeoman, a peasant? I did not pray to God in all that time. I heard the wind whistle across the long grass of the plains and looked onto the green horizon. Suddenly my choice seemed eternal, contemplating how to spend countless years on the endless plains of the Wyoming territory.

To start life anew, seemed like an odyssey across the sea of grass; *Am I a coward for seeking payment, when my soul is in turmoil?* I drank on it and sought no guidance.

Naturally, I was angry when a visitor came to my door. I wiped the dry crust from my mouth when I heard the knocking. After opening the door, I saw it was one of the messengers from the post office.

"I have a telegram for you," he said.

"From who?" I asked.

"The sheriff of Glengrove up north sent it down."

This was the usual way of requesting my services, fast and cheap. I hoped it was a case of mistaken identity or a message from a long lost relative, anything but that.

"Let me see that." I plucked it out of his hands. It was an abrupt and blunt request. "Need hangman, stop. Pay well, stop," it read.

"Thank you," I muttered as I closed the door. Glengrove was a half-day's ride away. I looked at the message again and wondered what would appear when I arrived. My bare house drove me to pack what I needed in the carriage. Looking out onto the green plains ahead of me, I emptied my lungs and slapped the reins to move forward.

After riding for several hours, my dried eyes suddenly opened. The town of Glengrove struck me instantly; it was the greenest place I had ever seen. The willow trees bordered the pond on the edge of town and waved their long, green limbs in the breeze. The rich color of the grass made it seem full of life. As I entered the town, the houses were painted white with pale columns and fences. The sheriff and his men appeared from the main road that cut the town in two. They slowed my horses. The sheriff approached. He wore a cavalry pin on his jacket and had a shaved head under his big hat. His smile lifted his square, white mustache as he patted my old horse on its back.

"You must be the hangman," he said.

"That's right."

"Follow us. I'll show you where we'll do it." He patted the horse again. "Make way!" He shouted.

The men split apart, making my path. The sheriff stayed beside me and guided me to a clearing on the other side of the houses. There was a tall tree in the center, towering over the town.

"There," he said with a pointed finger. "That should do it."

"Sheriff," I said. He kept pointing at the tree, walking ahead. "Sheriff!" I barked.

He turned around to face me. "What is it? Is the tree too tall?"

"I have what I need in the carriage. I'll build a scaffold for this."

"You don't need to do that. The tree will work."

"You don't understand what a hanging is supposed to do, do you, sheriff? There is a proper way to do this. I am acting on the power invested in me by the Wyoming Territory. This is a grave act."

He looked at me like I was a nuisance.

"Where is the prisoner?" I asked.

"I'll show you," he said with a sigh. "Tie your horses over there."

I roped the carriage to the tree. He waited for me with suspicious eyes. I slowly came to his side, and we made our silent march back to town.

When our feet met the main street, I realized that the townsfolk hadn't moved. They kept a path open for us and watched me. Some had smiles and others simply let their eyes trail after us. The sheriff led me into one of the large white houses with white columns.

The interior was open and empty. Well-cleaned wooden floors echoed our footsteps, and paintings of past relations hung along the walls. The light shined through heavenly crafted windows. It seemed strange that such a beautiful home was inside this small town. Through the open foyer was an office with a wide window, a dark desk, and a whiskey decanter. He poured a drink for me. I held it in my hand out of courtesy.

"Have you ever been to Glengrove?" He asked.

"No, I haven't."

"What do you think of it?"

"It's very nice." He sipped his drink and grunted in agreement.

"So where is the prisoner?"

"Do you have some sort of ritual you have to do before you execute a man?"

"I just like to know what they've done before going through with it."

"Ah, well you don't need to worry about that. I can tell you all about it."

"All right, what was his crime?"

"Dr. Orville was a very useful man around here. He brought in medicine and other remedies from Kansas. He healed people. At first, people liked him, but then his practice started to change. He began inventing his own medicine, and they trusted him all the same. He used his influence for the worse."

"What do you mean?"

"He was a charming man. A little too charming, if you understand my meaning."

"Tell me about it, all of it."

"Well, his medicine wasn't all that it was promised to be. One man fed this medicine to his donkey, and it died. He also sold a sort of balm that only he could place over affected areas, and well…to put it delicately, Dr. Orville was found to be committing adultery with another man's wife. That very same day, earlier in the morning, he prescribed a dose of his medicine to a dying man, saying it would help, and it killed him. We'd seen it work on others, but not this time. That's two counts of wrongful death and one count of adultery and several counts of medicinal malpractice."

"Is adultery a crime?"

"It's a sin," he insisted.

"That's correct, but not all sins are crimes in this territory."

"What good is the law if it doesn't punish sin?" He replied before finishing his drink.

"We might have everyone in prison then."

His faced hardened against me.

"When did this happen, these crimes?"

"It was yesterday."

"Yesterday, how did you have a trial in one day?"

"The evidence was clear."

"Where was the trial?"

"Here, in this house," he said.

"Is the prisoner here?"

"No, he's at the jail, but I wanted to bring you here to have a conversation."

"Then where is the judge?"

His face twisted. He had had enough of my questions. "We were his judge. We saw what he did and found him guilty."

"Sheriff, that is out of bounds. That is an unfair trial!"

"We have the evidence against him to find him guilty." A chilling feeling ran down my body. I set the glass down and stepped away from him.

"You need a judge and jury to try a man."

"He's a slippery one. We won't risk him leaving this town."

"So that he can receive a proper defense?"

"He's a swindler, do you understand? Swindlers have no place here."

"That may be, but every man needs a fair trial.

His guilt needs to be proven, not assumed."

"Look," he said tumbling his thumbs over each other. "You seem like a genuine, young man. A gentleman, if I may say. But you don't know this man like I do, like this town does. You don't know his sins."

"That's true, and you may be right about him, but you can't kill a man after being judged by a kangaroo court."

"He has been judged! This is the penalty for his crimes. This is your job!" He reached into the desk. His hand returned with a thick pouch. He gave it a small shake so that I could hear the low snap of coins inside. He threw it to me like it meant nothing.

"Do it," he said in a harsh whisper. I held my tongue. "Do it!"

I'd had enough. "Only after a rightful trial!" I turned and saw myself out.

The sheriff followed me and shouted commands. I paid no mind to his words, no matter how forceful. As I passed the center of town, the other townspeople followed. I heard scuffles and marching footsteps behind me. I turned and saw a thick crowd of them.

I didn't run, but I picked up the pace. I thought they would descend on me before I reached the tree, but I took hold of my horses undisturbed. I started to unbind my carriage from the tree, hoping they would simply escort me out of town.

I turned at the sound of laughter, hearty laughter at the defeat of a hated enemy. My hands did their work until the crowd grew closer. The sheriff knocked on the back of the carriage and showed himself. The others pooled in, surrounding the carriage.

"Bring in the prisoner," the sheriff's cavalier command rang out. Grass was swept underfoot from behind the carriage as three men brought forth the accused. The doctor was a portly man, late in life. His balding head was gashed, and he looked like he hadn't slept in days.

"Don't you know how to treat a prisoner?" I accused.

"We treated him like we should," one of his escorts declared.

"Maltreatment before a proper trial is unjust."

"We know what's just. This was just," he said. They shoved him at me.

His weight threw him down like an anchor. I hoisted him up by the arm. His dignity was gone, and his captors laughed and jeered.

"It's time for this to end," the sheriff said. "It's time to put your profession to good use."

"I won't do it."

"Bless you, young man," the doctor said.

"Quiet, you!" the sheriff barked.

"I didn't mean to poison anybody," he whispered to me. "I only wanted to help."

"I said that's enough!" the sheriff roared.

"The medicine I came with was gone. I had to invent my own instead. It was an honest mistake."

"No more begging from you, devil!"

"There is a judge in Cheyenne," I bargained. "I can take him there to receive his trial, and then I can continue with the execution if he is guilty of his crimes."

"He isn't leaving this town, and you need to make your choice."

"I have done wrong," the doctor whispered to me. "But don't let me die like this. Have mercy."

"Hangman!" The sheriff bellowed.

My eyes were latched to his, with calm disdain. "Fate will have its due. Do what needs to be done." I stood my ground. The wind blew over the green of Glengrove and cooled my back. The sheriff, red with rage, dug into the back of my carriage. Other men came closer, separating us from the horses. The doctor pressed his back against the tree, and I stood with him. The sheriff finally found the rope and held it out for me to take.

"You can't make me kill him," I said.

"This man must hang!"

"I'm not taking part in a lynching!"

From the corner of my eye, I saw a pistol fly from a holster. I stepped in front of the doctor, but the bullet cracked through his ribs before I could stop it. My hand feebly hung in the air. He gasped. He groaned. Another shot blew through him. My hand recoiled, and my eyes watched in impotence. Men were knocked into me, and my eyes sought for refuge. I threw myself onto the carriage and reached for the reins.

A pistol crack shocked me, and one of my horses collapsed to the ground. Its head was thrown back and it fell out of view. The sheriff was barking orders, but they were washed away by the grunts and groans of fighting men. I untangled my old horse from its reins and leapt on its back. I kicked it as hard as I could and leaned down against it. I'd never held onto anything as hard as I did those reins. Bullets flew past, and I flinched at every sound. The dense forest suddenly sheltered us and gave us time to escape.

Lost in the dark brush, I glanced around, looking for a path away from Glengrove. After charging through in blind haste, I had lost my way. I couldn't remember where the town was or where Cheyenne could be. I saw an opening beyond a patch of trees that could help me find a new path. There was a gap between the trees that I thought I could ride through, but my horse wouldn't go any further. It hissed and roared as the branches cut and poked its sides.

My feet hit the ground. My joints ached. I took a stick and struck a path for the horse. The reins strained between us. It still wouldn't go. *Come on, you dumb brute*. I pulled its reins and lurched backward into the open. The sun beat my tired back. I saw that the sun was beginning to fall. I threw my leg over my horse's back once more and followed it home.

## *Lamentations in the Wilderness*

With sore legs on top of my old horse, I was closer to home. The sun was starting to set. The soil turned red and brown. The trees had fallen behind me, and the fields were plowed and empty. Besides a white church along the road, there was no other landmark as far as I could see. The deeper the sun set on the horizon, the more I thought to see if anyone was inside. Perhaps a pew could be made into a bed for a traveler.

Before I could see into the church, a pastor in white robes opened the door. He kept his eyes on me. He held his hand in the air. I understood this was more than a friendly greeting. He knew I needed to rest. My whirling mind needed to hear a peaceful voice. I slowed my pace, raising my hand in return. His balding head and half-wrinkled face had shown a hard life, but his hands looked like they'd never lifted a finger.

"What can I do for you, pastor?" I asked.

He slowly lowered his arm, watching me with a serene expression.

"I think there is something I can do for you," he said.

I smiled and wiped my head.

"There is," I said on my way down off the horse. "I was wondering if you might have a spare cot for the night. I don't want to ride in the dark."

The pastor said nothing in response. His eyes narrowed, but not in suspicion.

"Can I spend the night inside your church, pastor? I will be out at dawn. I promise."

He measured me up with his eyes.

"I thought there was a reason that I should stay here this afternoon. I think it might be you."

"Well I am in need of some help. I can't make it back to town before dark."

"Of course, I have what you need. You can tie your horse to the post." He pointed to a black rod in the shape of a shepherd's crook. As I left my horse at the post, I noticed that he was watching me, hoping he could see something in me without a confession.

I followed him to the other side of the church. There was a narrow alley between the church and the cemetery. The low fence of the cemetery showed all the sleeping souls that belonged to that church; it was sure to grow in time. Behind the cemetery, and out of the shadow of the church, were two large stumps. There wasn't a tree around for several miles, as far as I could see.

I sat across from him on a stump and held my tongue. His eyes seemed to look right through me. His eyes, like his soul, were looking for some far-off destination.

"Where are you from?"

"Cheyenne, I came from Glengrove."

"What were you doing there?" He seemed genuine in his curiosity. His pleasant tone put me at ease.

"Working," I said, I had almost forgotten what had happened. Then I remembered. He could see my face darken.

"What is your profession?"

"Executioner, a hangman," I said.

His head rose and his shoulders leaned back.

"Yes, I had a feeling someone like you would

come this way."

"What do you mean by that?"

"I had a premonition, a feeling like something was incomplete. I had to stay behind to sort it out. You seem very tired. Has it been difficult traveling all this way alone?"

"Yes, it has. I go from town to town for my work."

"Does your work come with a heavy burden?" He asked, probing.

I had no words to describe how I felt. My turbulent soul had been churning over this question for so long.

"Do you have something you would like to tell me?" He asked.

I watched him. I wondered what made him so curious about me.

"I am a pastor, after all," he reassured me.

"I have some questions, yes," I said. My throat ran dry and I breathed deeply, mustering my courage. "I have done this work for years now...and I don't know if it's right. Is it right to kill a man for his crimes?"

The pastor considered my question. "God commands us to love our neighbor," he said.

"And I don't think I have for some time," I

confessed. "Shouldn't I show mercy to my enemies? Shouldn't I forgive those who have done wrong? If I don't, and stand as their judge at the gallows, does that make me cruel? If I judge others harshly, then I too will be judged. I can't bear that. I can't bear knowing that I may be one of them. I need to know. I need to put my mind at peace."

"Do you place your faith in God, our Lord Jesus Christ?" he asked.

"I do," I declared.

"Do you, a woeful sinner, beg merciful God to forgive you of your sins?"

"I do."

"Then you are forgiven of your trespasses," he said with a wave of his hand.

"Doesn't the Bible say that not all who call on God will be saved?"

"Yes, it does. But…"

"Then how do I know if He has forgiven me for what I have done? I have ended the lives of the guilty but not by the guidance of God. I have served judges who were corrupt as well as fair. I have done the most horrible things in the name of justice, man's justice, not God's." I sighed, defeated.

His eyes reflected my image. "Why do you do this work?" He asked. He was compassionate, unchallenging.

I was stunned that he would ask, and I thought of an answer. "My father was a hangman before me…is that my defense? If I am a good man, my actions should be to stay away from evil, no matter what family tradition may stand in the way. What do I do?"

The pastor was silent. My questioning didn't shock him. I was frantic, and these questions that I held for so long made me desperate.

"If I execute a man, am I in the wrong? Is taking another life for a sin I could also commit a sin as well? Can I be forgiven for it if that is my profession, if I feed myself by these deeds? And what if God allows this? What do I do then? If I don't execute the guilty, am I a coward?"

My hands gripped my knees. I feared hell's fire lashing my feet. My head snapped upward and saw his placid eyes holding their vision over my shaking body. He did not speak. I tried to coax him out of silence again.

"If I show mercy to wicked men, does God condemn me for abiding sin? The Lord says that we should forgive our enemies, but almost none of the men were my enemies, only strangers. Should I forgive them?"

"Yes, you should forgive your enemies."

"Then what should we do with them?" I asked. "We can't let them run wild. What do we do with the enemies of society? What do we do with the ones who may hurt or steal again?"

He was patient, listening all the while. His gaze, curious and kind, gave me hope for an answer.

"There are some men who should be taken away from society, until they are redeemed by God or serve their sentence," he said.

*Tell me what to do. What does God want from me?* I begged him for an answer. "What should I do? What should I do?"

He was touched by my eyes and came to my side. His arms cradled my shoulders.

"Our Lord laid down His life for your sins, my son. That is no small act. The burden on you weighs heavy because of your conscience. You are a redeemed sinner who must face his past. The tears of repentance can quench the fires of hell, my boy."

I shuddered in his arms.

"There is only so much bloodshed a man can bear. You don't have to do it anymore. Let go," he whispered.

He led me into the church; the white Gothic arch swallowed us into its candlelit sanctuary. We turned a pew around to face another, making a bed. Despite lying on that old wood, I fell into a deeper sleep than I can remember.

# *Epilogue*

Cheyenne was in bloom. It was rejuvenated. The bustling city was alive as if for the first time. The soft laughter of children fell on my ears. It warmed me to see that the whole city was out in the streets celebrating. The Wyoming Territory had achieved statehood. The balmy July sun covered us completely. I explored on my own in between the crowds. The mayor had invited me to speak with him. The cherry red faces of the townspeople were a sight for sore eyes.

A loud clatter came down from a wide street. A marching band played their tune and banners flew over them. They marched towards a platform before turning to excite other city folk. The platform was ornamented by flags, politicians, and policemen, all looking their best for the grand occasion. I swam past folks on my side of the street, looking for a space between horses and marching bands. When an opening came, I crossed the road and forced my way through those viewing the parade on the other side. Two policemen stopped me as I approached the platform with an absent-minded smile. The mayor saw me and trotted down the steps to intervene.

"Gentlemen, this is a guest of mine. You must not have met our reliable executioner." They curtly shook my hand. "I'm happy to see that you're here to listen to my speech. With men like you, we have finally civilized this land."

"Thank you," I said. He looked behind him and gestured to a rotund man.

"Meet this young man, Mr. Governor." He took heavy steps downwards to meet us. He towered over everyone. "This is our uh...hangman. He's done a lot to bring justice to this state." The governor grumbled and extended his hand. Tight and thick flesh wrapped around my hand. He pulled back as soon as the occasion allowed.

"It's good to see a man who loves law and order," he said. The mayor took him by the shoulder.

"I hope you enjoy the rest of the festivities," he said to me. "Stay close, you'll want to hear this speech of mine." His mouth lifted with a pearly grin and led the governor up the steps. Something stirred in me to speak up.

"I'm not a hangman anymore," I said.

The mayor turned on his heels. His face was dumbfounded.

"I'm sorry to disappoint you, sir. I've made up my mind. It has been an honor, and I look forward to hearing your speech." I gave him my hand and he shook it.

He was a bit dazed by it. "If you ever change your mind, we will still need men who believe in the law after today."

"I won't be changing my mind, but thank you, sir."

"What're you going to do?" He asked. He was concerned. The governor left us, clearly annoyed.

"I don't know." My smile grew wider. "I don't know what I'm going to do today or the next day or the day after that, but I know that I won't be doing what I have been doing ever again. I'm going to build things, sir. This land is changing and it's changing fast. There are going to be towns growing all over the state. I'll build anything I can dream of, and I'll know

I'll be doing something good." He was shocked to be charmed by my words; he grinned at this.

"We'll need men like you yet," he said. He tipped his hat.

I bowed my head slightly. I found space between the families watching the parade. The crowd surrounded me as it moved to follow the bands. I walked along with them, the trumpets buzzing in our ears.